JANET HOBHOUSE'S

NOVEMBER

NOVEMBER

JANET HOBHOUSE

VINTAGE CONTEMPORARIES

VINTAGE BOOKS · A DIVISION OF RANDOM HOUSE · NEW YORK

A Vintage Original, November 1986
First Edition
Copyright © 1986 by Janet Hobhouse

Library of Congress Cataloging-in-Publication Data

Hobhouse, Janet, 1948–
November.

(Vintage contemporaries)
"A Vintage original."
I. Title.
PS3558.03369N6 1986   813'.54   86-40148
ISBN 0-394-74665-1 (pbk.)

Grateful acknowledgment is made to Harper &
Row Publishers, Inc. for permission to reprint
four lines of poetry from "Archaic Torso of
Apollo" in *Selected Poems of Rainer Maria
Rilke*: A Translation from the German and
Commentary by Robert Bly. Copyright © 1981
by Robert Bly. Reprinted by permission
of Harper & Row Publishers, Inc.

Author photo copyright © 1986 by Jerry Bauer

Manufactured in the United States of America
10 9 8 7 6 5 4 3 2 1

For Robert Cornfield, Michael Shulan,
and Bruce Wolmer,
with love and gratitude.

NOVEMBER

Against the heavenly windowlight, a New England profile: solid line of brow and nose, mouth a little soft, soft eyes, brown. Zachariah Quine, strapped into his seat, on his way to London. So much and not much more was certain, certain only because out of his hands. His head was tilted to show that he was reading (this morning's *New York Times*), but he was not reading. Facing him head on you could see that his mind was elsewhere, captive of another consciousness, wrestling you'd say with whatever is left for twentieth-century man to consider a soul. Airborne, ungrounded, of no fixed abode. In search, was he? Not bored, certainly. All restlessness inside, body consciousness gone, aware of the border between self and companions only now and then, as now a girl rising to leave her seat pushed stockinged calves against his trousered knees. Looking up, he registered the pale apologizing face, and looking forward then, the T-shirted torso, twisting, inclined toward him as though to offer. A flinch-jolt of memory there, ghost of desire, banished by courtesy as they both withdrew: I did not mean to touch. Her body was younger than his, perhaps some twenty years. Looking, he remembered how this defined him (*Nel mezzo del cammin di nostra vita*—something—a dark wood). In his head he sometimes sprinted still, certainly asked the youthful questions: Where am I going and so on. Only now more and more: Where am I and all this baggage going? Accumulations from his life which he bore invisible among the carry-on luggage. They weighed him down, but were no anchor.

Paradoxical to feel the burden of what has been taken away. He had been free for three years. Maggie, taking Karen, had told him so. They were gone now, both of them, the connections snipped so that they might all dance into the future. Even the alimony payments, the silver thread that might have bound them, no longer accepted. Maggie made more money than he did, Karen's grandmother paid for school. And yet he did not feel free at all or lucky or footloose as they said he should. He felt thrown out of his life, useless because he was useless to them. What Maggie had called a prison had been sanity for him.

After three years? Still dazed? Still profligate, grieving. Still harping on his daughter. But he had tried. He had even believed Maggie about the freedom, and just after the divorce driven himself to the edge of experiment with six women and a haircut. He had left his job and cashed in his securities. He had moved from their large apartment into two small rooms downtown. And he'd been amazed in his freedom how little he really needed. He didn't need any longer a dining-room table and ten chairs, two bathrooms, a hallway; he didn't need a washer-dryer, his cameras, books, or suits. He took two cases, a bed, and his hi-fi equipment and began an uncluttered life. Only the Steinway, which he'd been forced to sell and which would not fit where he was going, did he miss. In its place he rented a small upright, and began work on an opera he'd been thinking about for years. In those first six months he canceled his magazine subscriptions, stopped taking his vitamins, accepted no invitations to dinner, concerts, or promotional cocktail parties. He took himself down to an imaginary line of just and no more than what was needed.

There followed a year of diminishing conviction of heroism. The opera was abandoned and a journal begun, the journal abandoned and a systematic program of reading begun, the reading abandoned and a program of television watching begun and adhered to, leading to Zach's understanding that what was needed was a point to his existence. In eighteen months he had made himself a tabula rasa, with nothing to do and no one to do it with.

All right, he had said, a perfect place to start. He would learn everything from scratch like a noble savage. How to live. He was free, wasn't he?

From some still mysterious fuse point deep inside their marriage, they had careered away from each other like human cannonballs, Maggie progressively discovering herself by a series of understandings of her limits. What I am not, will no longer do. I am *not*, she said at one time or another during the months preceding the divorce, your mother, your daughter, your sounding board. I am *not*, she said on friendlier occasions, with reference to her acting career, just anybody, an ingenue, part of the Pepsi Generation. Whereas for Zach to know what he was not would have been the greatest possible help. At the moment, and rather suddenly, he was no longer husband, father, employed, or altogether stable.

No rules, no constraints. He didn't even have habits he could depend on. After years of healthy living, he discovered in himself cravings for cheap food: fast-fried chicken and cupcakes. Not even real cupcakes, but the kind that approximated nothing and were squashed in the packet when you bought them, icing and plastic wrapper tasteably fused from months on the shelf. In the past he had chosen wine carefully, imagining himself something of a connoisseur, going to wine auctions, hunting through bin-ends at out-of-the-way importers. Now he drank California Barolo, and by the barrel. Barolo with everything: fish, pastrami, oatmeal. Oatmeal was one surprise, for supper, with wine and cupcakes to follow. He no longer got hangovers, which was another surprise. After years of caution with the spirits, he found he could drink what he wanted: ouzo, Spanish brandy. Zach was smoking, too, mentholated Marlboros. And for exercise only the pacing around his room between bouts of creativity, later only the trips to the bathroom during commercials on daytime TV. He might have supposed his body— at forty—would object to this life. But it just went on, trustingly, systematically poisoned, slacker but no heavier, and without the warning signs Zach three years ago would have expected to see. Not even a heart murmur to tell him this wasn't the way. If there were rules as to how to live, his body wasn't aware of them. Or so it seemed.

On the other hand, some things that he was sure he could count on had secretly slipped away. When the hi-fi equipment was stolen, he discovered he'd let his insurance payments lapse; he fell behind with his rent and paid his Blue Cross twice. He bounced checks at the cleaners and locked himself out. After fifteen years of looking after Maggie and Karen, he discovered himself to be something of an idiot with regard to money. This too was a surprise, and made him nervous.

It should have humbled him. He should have welcomed the chance to learn how to live, as a child, without old habits, old convictions. Yet he remained obstinate, sure that at bottom there was a certain order, a stopping place, something that was part of him that was *not* a surprise, and that under the dust storm of shifting circumstance, there was something sound inside him that knew what was right and would give his life its meaning.

"Why does man imagine he is made for happiness?" some TV pundit asked him at four A.M. as he sat over his bowl of cornflakes.

"Because he is!" Zach shouted back. And there he voiced surprisingly loudly his remaining conviction, the last and deepest instinct he felt still able to count on.

By the following summer he might not even have whispered as much. He had taken his life so far down he'd forgotten the original purpose of the descent. Through the summer heat he lay under the cheap air conditioning drinking iced Barolo and refusing to answer the phone. With Karen away at camp, he was spared even his weekend obligations of cleanliness and sobriety. Deprived of his daughter's visits, he succumbed in a haze of game shows and old movies. He might even have imagined himself content, certain that things would change, that he was going through some stage necessary for rebirth in the autumn. One day/ night that summer he had risen from his bed, dressed in his socks and underpants, and gone to the bathroom, still chuckling over the comedy of a soft-drink commercial. Looking through himself in the mirrored cabinet—unable lately to take the image straight on—he had heard noises coming from inside. Opening the door slowly, and like part of some horribly scripted commercial himself, he had seen his own razor blades, worse, heard them, singing like the Andrews Sisters. Cavorting and dipping and trilling, like mermaids in the shallows, they had sung to him: "Come, come to me." They were not, Zach knew, referring to the beard, but to the whole package. They were offering an answer.

Eighteen years ago, another flight, homeward, back from luxurious exile. Fleeing England, Zach had headed for New York. New York was where you did things that mattered. He was American but that was not the point. New York was the point: a society of solo fliers, all on separate flight paths, gliding into private destinies, living out the true loops and curves of unique lives, life itself conceived as spiritual adventure—at least in his crowd: bohemians engaged in fiction, painting, "the dance." Neither money nor fame was a motivation, but to learn what your own voice was and then sing with it, to take part in the honored chorus, the erotic hum of dedicated individuals—that was everything. And for that they were willing to substitute for the commonly lived reality that other reality, those private structures of art that could be sustained only with the greatest daily sacrifices, a perverse faith, and inhuman amounts of solitude.

Who were they? Waitresses who had once played Portia, Helena, Juliet at expensive universities; taxi drivers who parked their cabs in front of fire hydrants and ran upstairs to show slides of their work to galleries; salesmen, graduate students like Zach, who moonlighted long nights on novels that would work like alchemy to make universal myths out of the wounds and boredom of childhood. Each life guarded its secret shape, guessed at the curve of its own vine, monitored its inner workings inside a silence drastically imposed on the noises of that other, fraudulent "real" world. Heady stuff all that parade of art allegiance, the vaunting of sacrifice, displays of indifference to conventional values. How pompously they used to wear their secondhand clothes, as though the stains were medals for money not spent on laundries, stripes for valor in the face of department-store seduction. Money existed only to let you continue; beyond that it was there for paperbacks, foreign films, and the drink that brought you near the muse, and if not the muse, then some bar girl in black miniskirt with an analyst or a yoga teacher or a first edition of Djuna Barnes. No one paid a decent rent, but then hardships, hallway muggings, un-heated apartments, were only signs that, things being dan-gerous, the pilgrims were on the right road. Zach's two years in England, the summer evenings, the long light on college lawns, flowerbeds littered with champagne corks—what was that to the real thing, the New York life that followed?

It had seemed peculiarly American, the opportunity and the freedom, the melting-pot chaos in which private des-tinies could flourish. It was the fervor of pursuit that was special to the city, religious almost, zealous, a holier form of the free-for-all that had been offered immigrants for dec-ades. New York was a Yukon-Salem where you could get spiritual riches, save yourself, and flee, one way or another, a kind of poverty and death. So it had seemed to Zach flying westward eighteen years ago. So it no longer seemed. Case histories. Friends. Christopher, chess-playing recluse and forager, surviving among the hookers in his rent-free, heat-free room in Hell's Kitchen, nothing to steal but ripped off anyway, tied up with telephone cord, burned with cigarettes. And Belle, Vassar dropout in fishnet tights, swallowing everything the sixties offered—men, pills, philosophy—had flipped sideways and taken herself home. And Alice, poet, breaking through, feted, had one day just stopped, self-described as finished, desiccated by the solitude, too "orig-inal" for ordinary life, misfitted by and hostage to her own career. Or Zach himself, hedging his bets as composer/ teacher, and old believer in the great doctor's prescription, Freud's "love and work," thinking that with Maggie he didn't have to choose, that there could be adventure taken by two as pure as the solitary tramping, but himself abandoned by Maggie in pursuit of her freedom, their life together renamed her bondage. And now Maggie lost among the women that saw men as the enemy, bringing up Karen that way, Zach shunted, set free.

He no longer wished to be unique. It seemed a ludicrous idea to him, as much a burden as those pressures on him as a young man to conform. He wanted, though he feared he might no longer know how, to crawl back into the camp of the human tribe. He wanted *their* wisdom now, how to live, and the warmth he imagined to exist beyond the series of doors he'd slammed with such arrogance in his youth. Humbled, all of forty, Zach was heading back, U-turning midair like some brained homing pigeon, convinced of nothing except that he was no longer strong enough to fly. Anywhere, any piece of firm ground would do.

Across the aisle, a middle-aged Indian in Hong Kong silk suit shot a bony-wristed brown hand in and out of his cuffs as he addressed his companion.

"It is all," he said, his voice breaking into the hum of the plane and cracking in the manner of a child on the verge of tears, "entirely a question of how we choose, yes I am telling you, *choose* to see things. Let me give you an example."

"Please," said the younger man.

"In front of us is a baby, am I not right?" He nodded towards an infant two rows ahead of them. It had struggled over the arm of its parent, and was now staring mournfully at the passengers behind, while sucking on the corner of the plastic headrest.

"We say this baby is one year old, do we not?" the Indian went on.

"Perhaps more," said his friend.

"Never mind, that is not my point. We say 'one year old' and yet one year is not old. Even for a baby it is not old. Why should we not say 'one year young'? Do you see my point?"

"Oh yes," said the younger man.

"It is always like this," said the Indian, "we let the language think for us. Let me tell you about the miracle of Jesus and Lazarus."

"Please," said his companion.

"You know the story of this miracle. Jesus says to Lazarus: 'Lazarus, get up. Get up from the dead.' And Lazarus gets up from the dead. Well anyone can *say*, 'Get up. Get up from the dead.' That is not a miracle. But for Lazarus to get up from the dead, *that* is a miracle. It is not Jesus but Lazarus who makes the miracle."

"Oh yes," said his companion.

"It is my belief that we are all this Lazarus," the Indian said, "and we can all do this miracle."

"Listen, Zach," Anita had said to him that summer, "it's all in here." Anita was a dancer, working nights to finance herself through a Psychology M.A. Still in her show gear, trailing cat tails down her black-leather jumpsuit, she had pressed upon him a volume of Melanie Klein.

"You're still in the Narcissistic phase," she said to him. "You haven't made it to the Depressive."

"I think you could say I had," Zach said.

"That's what she calls it, a point of wisdom, when the infant can accept that just because the mother's breast is gone, it doesn't mean it's gone forever. You still think there are two breasts, Zach," Anita told him patiently, "one good one that comes, one bad one that goes. But there's only one, one good one that comes and goes. The good tit returns," Anita told him, "believe me."

Zach read the book and tried to understand life in terms of Manichaeism and mastectomy. Translated into the language of his old Eng. Lit. courses, it seemed to come down to a requirement of Negative Capability. He should be patient and faithful and wait quietly for the return of good luck and his love of life.

When he'd finished the book, he called Anita, picturing to himself *her* good breasts returning—in their evening wraps, the little silver tassles that hung like tears from Anita's childish body.

"The business about the breasts is more complicated than I thought," she said. "We've been reading Otto Rank." And she explained to him while his desires dropped to his ankles and the truth sank in. The business about the breasts was that he was, they all were, doomed. It wasn't simply a question of whether this breast was going to come back or not, but whether it would be entirely welcome when it did. Desire for union conflicted with desire for freedom. The choice was between love and claustrophobia or independence and loneliness. This all rang familiar; he'd heard it often enough from Maggie. You'd never win, whether you got what you wanted or not. Having it was its own problem.

"Otto Rank says there are no solutions," Anita said solemnly, "only temporary unions, a lot of guilt, and general neurosis." This too seemed a reasonable view.

"However," Anita went on, "there's a coda on the Artist. He's the only one Rank has any hope for. It's not quite clear how it happens, 'a triumph of Will and Deed,' he says, but the Artist [by which Anita certainly meant herself, possibly Zach as well] is able to sublimate this conflict through his art. Art, Zach," Anita said, "is your answer."

"I should go back to the opera."

"As fast as you can. As for myself, I am off to dance my troubles away."

"At the Pepper Pot?"

"Rank does not discriminate among the circumstances under which Art is made."

Zach returned to the opera. For six weeks he rose early, as though to steal a march on the legitimate working population of New York, and while from under the cartoon cubism of its skyline the city blinked its artificial light, Zach tapped out small melodies on the rented piano.

The opera told the story of a young agoraphobe who fantasizes about his unseen neighbors' lives and discusses them with the objects in his room. Zach scored parts for his bed and coffee grinder, wrote tangos for his shoes, water music for the pipes in the bathroom. After several weeks' work he played the first sketch through. It sounded like some of the cuter ads he'd been watching on television. And it was too cheerful to describe anyone's life. If he could have had at least some conviction of the formal significance of what he was doing, some sense that he was breaking new ground . . . But he was stuck with the postmodernist free-for-all and its accompanying malaise: where anything goes, most things did, it seemed to Zach, so that the subject matter had to carry the whole purpose of the work. *Pace* Rank, Zach had no desire to tell his own story, let alone the story of his furniture. The idea was to sublimate neurosis in art, not to celebrate it.

"Of course, you can't work here," his sister Dinah told him during a brief visit from Florence. She sat on his bed, holding a catalog of a recent drawing exhibition, dressed unseasonably in a suit of dark red velour, wearing little Turkish embroidery shoes.

"I'm only here one week and I feel shot through with speed. Even if you never go out, Zach, this place has to get to you. Listen to that street noise." Zach could no longer hear it.

"Well, read the papers then. Look at this Tylenol business. Some crackpot puts arsenic in the pain-killer. People read about it, decide it sounds like a fun idea. Copycat murderers, the press says, as though they were naughty children. And what's Halloween now? Razor blades in the apples, poison in the candy. New York is terminal, Zach, face it. Why do you think Michael stayed in England? Why do you think Europe's crawling with New Yorkers? The rats are abandoning ship. They don't want to be poisoned; they don't want to be stabbed; and those are just ordinary people. You think an artist if he had the choice would choose this place?"

He would and he did. New York was lousy with artists.

In the end, it wasn't the speed or the sickness that drove Zach from the city, it was to get away from all the artists. All those Sohoites in grim fatigues, all those filmmakers, dancers, potters, sonneteers, all those weavers and acrobats, conceptual and performance artists, all those individualists living in cells—waking to the sound of their own callings, facing East to them daily, bending at the altars of their own separateness and freedom. If there was anything to this breast and artist business it was that, far from sublimating the conflict between connection and solitude, the artist had simply pushed the breast churlishly and fatally from his jaws. Between the breasts, then, Zach would no longer seek salvation in art or love—which according to Rank and verified by Zach's recent experience—was only a kind of Tylenol, at best temporary relief, possibly poisoned. Nor would he sit there patiently waiting for the Good Breast to return. He would seek it out, the great warm bosom of the ordinary world, throw himself upon it, and suck.

But no, Zach said to himself now, nothing is done in exasperation, despair more like, utter humiliation of ignorance acknowledged.

The plane glided through iridescent clouds. Evening sun caught silver wingtip and broke over the edge into fiery lines. A blessing somewhere, breaking in on metal, plastic, tweed. And something broke in him: Beauty, Necessity, he said, is out there.

ondon. Home of his brother Michael, once home to him. He stopped when the city hit him, the other side of the glass doors. Taxis, buses. That color of damp sidewalk, the secretive way the light struck, puddles everywhere, pigeons strolling ankle-deep in them. A peculiar odoriferous gray to it, and beyond the gray, green in damp, overpowering opulence. And the littleness, toyness of the shapes: fat, square cabs, red lozenge buses. He was lost in someone's nursery. The sudden safety of the place overwhelmed him. He'd forgotten so much. He *knew* this place. He saw his companions from the plane, sanitarily wrapped in their traveling clothes, trim skirts and short raincoats. The sad propriety of that matching luggage, the American footwear on uneasy, shifting feet: already nervous of the foreign place, the rules already confusing: QUEUE THIS SIDE FOR TAXIS. *Queue*, pretty foreign word for the promised common culture, you couldn't even pronounce it. Zach pitied, gloated, almost sprang, impatient for London that still was his. He'd bought it twenty years ago and it had bought him; he heard these winnings like the spew of a slot-machine, a crash of coinage as the familiar images embraced him: the cheap construction of the English bus shelter, the cab drivers, obsequious still, reading evening papers inside smoke-reeking compartments, the noise of those cabs, dieseling like a lullaby. Zach stood still and took it in. Twenty years he thought he got back in these first minutes out of the airport, standing in the fresh, damp air of the London evening.

He wished now he hadn't booked the tourist hotel; it seemed to him the taxi could simply take him home. Even the last trip with Maggie, blanked out in a haze of spending and rushed visits, was made nothing in this sudden reconnection.

His cab drove up. Omen or hallucination, he heard himself addressed as *guv'nor*. He humped his suitcase inside and followed it, onto the luxurious backseat, room enough for a family of ten.

Maybe it was just the tourist thrill, not the homecoming. He tried to imagine a Paris ride, the hair-thinning chase through narrow streets, the surly local, hunched malevolent inside an unsprung Citröen, large ancient, glaucomaed, foul-breathed Alsatian up front with the driver so that you risked your hand when you paid. Tip scrutinized, exact doorstep delivery declared *impossible*, the crawl out from the broken banquette, luggage thrown on pavement. But even that could make you happy. It was familiarity. It was the reminder that you had lived, been somewhere before, a promise of more life in reconnection with the past. You got things back again. It was possible to think that nothing was really ever lost for good.

Riding in from the airport, Zach stared through his window at the mean red Edwardian housing: long terraces, closeness, people needing to lean together. And trees everywhere. Green. Nature insisted on: the English right to a garden. Some things were new to Zach, not so life-insisting. Not much of a grip on modern architecture, beyond the understanding it ought to be tall. But no light in the stone, no life and no finish. A halfhearted acquiescence to the times. In America, the future was still imagined as an ally. The English had no reason to trust it, and said so: We need not go yet, joyless, deprived. They just deposited those buildings, like some tax ungraciously paid, with space on either side of the structures where the eye could pass, censor the foolish rhetoric, and get on with normal life.

They said that in England people living in high-rises became unstable, suffered breakdowns. It went against the grouping nature, deprived them of the traditional sooty companionships of back-to-back housing. In America, separateness was the premium, the frontier heritage: blow your brains out for trespassing. The skyscraper was the way out for Manhattan Island; if you can't get away, you get up. No nervous breakdowns, those were for the streets. Up there, all was clean and grandiloquent: the long vistas, stars and skyline, the worship of the possible in the long, undirtied view.

English energies were spent on preservation, a blind clinging to the given: the huge, ugly Victoriana. Not the New York way—when something was finished you ripped it down.

Not much longer, Zach thought; Americans would have to learn to take up less room. It was no preservation society, though, even the homeless burned down their homes—the South Bronx. But that was something else: "Jewish lightning," they called it, arson for insurance.

The English clutched at the past, cowered there. And Zach had come to cower with them.

He was tired now, from the flight, or the fear, perhaps, as he got used to London, that its promise would go. He thought he smelled of travel, or of his recent life: the waft that loonies have of body disconnection. Michael tomorrow. The hotel would have a bathroom like a royal chamber: English plumbing, hot water, radiators, tea poured down in pints for body heat. He remembered now the awful damp at Oxford and the firm of plumbers, Thomas Crapper and Sons. English jokes, and that thing the doctors asked you: "How're the waterworks?"

The taxi racketed along the highway. And then suddenly they entered it, the darkened town. Marble Arch, cinema lights, Park Lane, turning in, no one on the streets, lighting dim, Mayfair. Stop. Here.

The man at the registry desk was slow, and irritable, as though preempting that response in his customers. His tunic was immaculate, a dense purple on which two lines of brass gleamed, catching the lights that were all around the hotel entrance, in the glass partitions and the polished wood, on the marble floors and porcelain pots. His eye, though, was dead, projecting weariness that was infectious. Behind him, a team of younger staff occupied themselves in ceremony, sluggishly. Their own sense of time here, nothing precious about it. Zach waited inside the Edwardian static. It was clean, but not brisk, nothing like the urgency of New York, rude often, premised on a notion that time was flying. Weather was faster too, both the heat and the rain. Here the weather, like the place, promised you could live forever.

A small bellboy, ludicrous in his cap with string under chin, like an organ grinder's monkey, took Zach's case and led him to the lift. The same age as Zach's daughter, job-harnessed, underfed, he carried himself like an old man, called him Sir, seriously, begrudging no one. Zach felt the boy's humiliation but, implicated in the charade, acted his part, tipped him, and connived at the uniformed imposture.

Alone in his room, he sensed it mysteriously empty, glossily silent. New York ghosts threatened from the luggage. He would unpack tomorrow. London was gone again. He found his whiskey and sleeping pills, drank his oblivion from a tooth mug, started to sleep in the shower, crawled to bed.

He woke suddenly and with too much clarity in the morning, already alert to the nervousness that had been his customary New York greeting of the day: the anxious treading of air before a heart-stopping descent to his ground of hopelessness. By hellish engineering the wires were connecting him even now, fastening him into this anxious present, slide-bolting him into his past. He regretted the absence of anesthesia. Too tired to do the job properly last night, he was this morning defenseless, vulnerable to just such an ambush.

But not quite clear. Waking, he listened for the sounds that would place him in the morning in New York: trucks from Long Island farms hitting potholes on their way up-town, the crash of metal accordion gates opening the hard-ware store on the street below, the thump of dried pulp and newsprint as the papers, bound in nylon rope, hit the sidewalk, farewell shouts of the all-nighters. From his present position he heard nothing but a distant motor on the ground below, footsteps passing on the carpeting outside his door, and lowered English voices, clipped, considerate, content, on their way to the lifts, to breakfast, to pleasantly start the day.

Zach moved to join them. He roused himself with the name of where he was, understood he must know himself in a different city, woo himself into a different future.

He followed the stairs down and ordered the elaborate hotel breakfast. He took tea from an ancient waiter, watched as the hot, polished containers were set before him on the starched white cloth, one by one, next to the gleaming curlicued rack that held cold warping triangles of scraped and crustless toast, next to the silver pot of butter rising yellow in a perfect convex, next to the jars that held dense speckled jams and bitter, lustered marmalade. Offered these things: the silver pots of water, milk, the teapot itself, scaled for one, with stained, heat-curled paper ends of Lipton tea bags hanging on crooked strings; presented with waxed rolls and eggs glistering in rigor mortis under a silver-domed dish, served cups and plates and numerous utensils; and placed above the array in a velvet armchair that bit into a thick dust-smelling carpet as the palest of morning lights entered and simultaneously died inside the room, Zach felt himself present at an elaborate and significant exam. Coping with his breakfast, measuring its pace, responding ritually to the ritual before him, he had the illusion of his own mastery, of the clarity of the challenge.

For this he prolonged his meal, smoking his cigarettes and reordering tea until the dining room gradually emptied and the breakfast dishes were removed, and the waiters began to chat with one another, working around him, joking, ignoring him, the ceremonies abandoned. He passed through to the lounge, steadying himself still for his entry into London. In the collapse between the end of breakfast and eleven-o'clock coffee, while an old woman in a nylon apron vacuumed the crested carpets, around and beneath the feet of patrons reading leather-bound reports of country life, Zach sat in a mahogany phone booth and called his brother.

Michael chose the restaurant and Zach was late. Nothing odd about that: their characteristic two-step. Zach only gives Michael the lead so he can trip him up. Zach remembered how this pattern existed all through their childhood, with Dinah hovering somewhere in the background, trying to get a sisterly foot in the door. But basically it was the Zach-and-Mike show, all those times Zach would ask advice of Michael, confessing over the Wheaties, seducing the brotherly wisdom, and then—wump: Never let them forget, however nice, however lost he seems, Zach is the special one; you can tell by the way he breaks the rules.

And here they were again, though both of them were pushing forty, with kid-brother Michael still ready to help, still pumping love and patience, and Zach still falling apart at the seams.

Zach walked on old floorboards down a soup-stained red carpet, silently girding himself, coaxing: For Christsake, don't let him think this is some *Reader's Digest* identity crisis.

Michael was capable of a less-than-believable, somewhat static, sympathetic expression, a kind of greed for funerals, which this moment Zach dreaded seeing. Right now, there was no expression at all, only the top of Michael's sparsely covered head as he scrutinized the menu. Michael had insisted on meeting here, a fancy and pretty touristy place, *olde worlde*, but one they'd used to frequent when it was cheaper, when, twenty years ago, they came up to London weekends, two dapper Fulbrights in seersucker and white bucks, overjoyed by English life and a favorable rate of exchange. Zach's arrival brought Michael out of his tassled reading matter. He grinned and hovered, then pushed back his chair, rose and grabbed his brother. An un-English greeting, prolonged and noisy. "Baby," Michael said when he let go of him, "this is some amazing sight."

They stared at each other, swaying and grinning like Labradors. "Sit down," Michael said, "I'll get you a drink. What happened, you couldn't get a cab?"

"Overslept," Zach said feebly. He was aware that he was already lying, keeping a distance. Three thousand miles to get here, and the last inches fought.

"So you missed your kippers." Zach did not correct him. "What are you doing in that fancy hotel? You could have come to us straight from Heathrow. As a matter of fact you could have given us some warning, you can afford the calls."

They touched on this subject lightly and veered off. Zach had been bad at keeping contact, and Michael had never felt able to disturb him, break into whatever it was that kept him silently preoccupied in New York. About once every six months a short letter would come from Zach, and Michael would write back at length, ten, twelve pages each time, a bulky package with photos, a child's drawing, marginalia by Michael's wife, Helen, sometimes a news clipping with Michael's sarcastic expatriate remarks, each time an overflowing bundle from Britain, Michael's loving response to Zach's parsimonious communication.

"What do you want?" Michael asked as the waiter came up to them. "Remember they refuse to understand the cocktail here. Whiskey sours still taste like lemonade. Have whiskey straight or what, you tell me."

The waiter stood to one side, pretending not to listen. He was a senior, Hungarian, the juniors were mostly Spanish. In London restaurants you got the same kind of ethnic ascent you used to get in New York or Chicago, where every twenty years some group would make it safely to American invisibility: first the Germans and the Irish, then the Italians and Poles, last and not so easily done, of course, the blacks. The Hungarian with his thin moustache and chalky face was in charge now, but when Zach and Michael first came to this restaurant he'd have been treated as much like a cretin as the present group of accented underlings. The headwaiter in those days would have been impeccably, a little impatiently, English, or possibly fake French.

"Scotch, no ice," Zach said.

"A double whiskey," Michael told the waiter. "You've forgotten a lot," he said to Zach. "Ice is still regarded as a foreign gimmick, and the whiskey measure wouldn't coat a mosquito."

"I thought something might have changed," Zach said, "in all these years."

"This is England," Michael said happily. "Change is only for countries with something to gain by it. You think they have microchips in heaven?"

"You still think this is heaven?" Zach asked him.

"I still think it's pretty good." Michael pulled back a little from the questioning, handed Zach a menu. "Choose," he said, "so we can find out why you're here."

In fact, Michael chose, impatient for Zach to come out from behind the red boards. "I can't wait all day for this," he said, signaling the waiter. "Basically you want fish or meat? Have the Dover sole."

"All right," Zach said, "but no grapes or cheese." That was an old joke they had, about another restaurant, specializing in sole with fifteen, and to the Americans all outrageous, sauces. They had called the place Howard Johnson's after the American chain that offered twenty-eight flavors of ice cream.

"OK. Why are you here?" Michael said, leaning forward, after the waiter was gone.

"That's nice, some brotherly greeting."

"Answer the question."

"How are Helen, the kids?"

"Great, we did that on the phone. How are you, Zach, you look a little rough."

"Am a little rough," Zach said simply.

Michael waited. His face went into that look, prematurely grieving.

"Dinah said I should come. Thinks I should get out of New York."

"Dinah? Since when have you listened to Dinah? How is she? Still wearing a beret?"

"Still wearing a beret."

"What about your job?"

"Gave it up," Zach said, "eighteen months ago." That was the hardest thing to tell Michael, the most wanton of his acts.

"Everyone's chasing tenure and you give it up?"

"Before they gave me up," Zach said.

"Jesus," Michael said, "is it that serious?" Michael looked at him, cocking his head like a bird. "I thought you got through that mess with Maggie, came out the other side."

"Sure I did. Tunnel vision, day by day, and pretty soon you're skating. You know how it goes, you throw away your old clothes, fuck everything that moves, think you're free and happy and wonder how you could take the other as long as you did. Then you nose-dive. I did. Then I thought I pulled out. I started to work on some music, something I started years ago, an opera."

"Oh God," Michael said.

"Yeah, well. In the end that wasn't the problem."

"So what exactly are you living on?" Michael asked him.

"Not a lot, the Steinway, a few investments, some notion I'll figure it out eventually."

"Fish?" The waiter brought Zach his sole and replaced the cutlery.

"What's this?" Zach said, picking up a blunt, scalloped instrument.

"Don't you remember?" Michael said, "That's a fish knife." He hesitated, weighing his loyalties, then handed Zach's knife to the waiter. "My brother prefers the other kind," he said politely. "Victorian invention," he told Zach. "Pretentious, utterly useless."

"Thanks," Zach said. "Listen Michael, I'm OK, I just want to see what else goes on, a few alternatives."

"To what?"

"To sitting in New York, watching my life shrink like a shirt."

"I thought you went to California for that. Forget it," Michael said, as the waiter poured their wine, "I'm glad you're here, for whatever reason. And Dinah's probably right, London's a good, soft place to land. You see this?" He shoved his finger at Zach's plate. "They still have little hairnets on the lemons. Cute, huh? Well, welcome to London." He raised his Muscadet to his brother. "Helen's dying to see you."

She opened the door, momentarily dazzling him with the bright light of the hallway. He stood on the steps, smiling foolishly, blinking, hovering on the stone.

"Hello, Zach," Helen said. She kissed him on the cheek and let him in, led him to the back of the house and downstairs to the kitchen. Objects vaguely edible hung from the ceiling and twisted round the windows. Beyond, the garden, large, soft, living, pressed into the room in a kind of reverse heliotropism, as though the things growing there could hardly wait to get inside, be caught, preserved, eaten. Along the walls of the kitchen, in the spaces around the open pine shelving, where ghosts of former meals clung to the wood—the vague odors of garlic, coriander, coffee, mint from the garden—were children's drawings. On the sideboard, a large tawny cat slept inside a blue china bowl.

It was growing dark, but Helen stood with the door to the garden open and gave Zach a glass of wine. He watched her as she moved around the kitchen, idly, content. She

seemed to him unchanged by the years since he'd seen her:
the same private gravity, the same North Oxford manner
of dress—tonight, a green paisley blouse and dark wool skirt
of uncertain era, the clothes unacknowledged and shapeless
on her. Zach saw again the legs, still stunning, and the
smile: Helen's good teeth, good nature. She spoke to him
now as though they'd barely been separated, moving slowly,
seamlessly, like a person in a dream, lightly handling what
she touched, glass bottles, wooden board, small pots from
the refrigerator, moving things from one place to another,
aware of a private order, secret priorities inside the profu-
sion. Zach watched her, unable to distinguish her from the
silent, sensual dance, impressed by the slowness and contentment. With a pang, he acknowledged that Michael had
made her happy.

From upstairs, a child's voice descended as it talked to a
dream, excited, unfrightened. Helen stopped to listen, apologized, and went upstairs. Zach, alone in the big room,
wandered, looking, touching things: old copies of the *New
Statesman*, a brightly colored children's book, laminated,
a necklace of infant toothmarks strung along one corner.
He picked up a pencil that lay over two photographs: one
of a children's birthday party, the other, a couple Michael
and Helen's age, on a boat, dark, smiling fiercely.

The cat followed Zach's movements with suspicion and
then as though offended, leaped from its bowl and fled the
room, low-bellied along the floor. Zach filled his wineglass
and sat on a wheel-back chair to wait for Helen's return.
All the wood in the kitchen made for small, constant noises,

shifting and sighing. Something man-made purred and ticked erratically; a humming came from inside the walls. All that sound seemed to have connection with Helen, and all her Orphean power had something, Zach was not sure how much, to do with his brother. Remembering Helen's mother, Zach thought how easy it would have been for her to grow differently. That time, twenty years ago, when Zach had gone with Michael to meet them: Michael's tutor at college and his family. He could remember her mother's brittle chatter defenseless against her father's silence. The chirp and constancy of it so out of step with what was actually there during that bare uncomfortable meal that even he, Zach the foreigner, with his knife in the wrong hand and his exotic vowels, seemed more at home than that nervous lady. Zach remembered how she spoke into silence about Oxford matters, roses, Michael and Zach's Americanness, which had seemed to her to mean a kind of physical endowment:

"Of course with all your wonderful weather, it's not surprising you make such brilliant athletes. I suppose you're able to play tennis all year round."

"Actually, in Massachusetts, the winters are pretty harsh."

"Do try to listen, Margaret."

"Well, skiing, then," she'd said sweetly.

"The Fulbright awards are not given for athletics, Margaret."

"Of course not."

"I don't believe I can finish this," Michael's tutor had said as he left them. "Why don't I join you later?" Even on that night, Zach had been sorry that his kind, unathletic brother, in rescuing Helen, had not been able, likewise, to rescue her mother.

Helen came downstairs, holding a small, soft toy in one hand.

"Everything all right?" Zach asked her.

"Mick wanted to know whether you'd come yet and when he could see you. I got him to sleep again, I hope you don't mind."

"Of course."

"And where is Michael?" Helen looked up at the kitchen clock, loudly painted but silent, its guts removed by modern surgery, replaced by quartz.

"I was remembering when I first met you," Zach said to her.

"That must be more than twenty years ago, an unimaginably long time."

"Unimaginable, looking at you now," Zach said, "you've hardly changed."

"Oh, I have," Helen said quietly. "But then I've had an easy life." This was tribute to Michael, or was it merely true?

"How are your parents?" Zach tried to remember if Michael had written anything. Death? Divorce wasn't likely.

"Flourishing," Helen said. A voice from a time when age and extinction didn't happen to people you knew. "My father's head of another college now. He complains about the wine cellar and their having to admit women, but they've forced him to move with the times."

33

"And your mother?"

"Terribly well," Helen said. She gave Zach the rest of the wine and redirected the conversation, "Are you starving?"

"No, I'm fine." Everyone was fine. Everyone's parents and everyone's selves. All fine.

"I can remember your father telling me he read *Paradise Lost* in the bath," Zach said, not knowing why he remembered this, "and I remember being shocked."

"He was showing off," Helen said affectionately. "I can just imagine him, testing you. I suppose he thought you being American, New England, you would somehow be Puritan, that Milton would be your official bard."

"I think I was more shocked by your father's display of familiarity, or impressed. Perhaps I imagined him soaking a first edition."

"Now *that* would have been sacrilege," Helen said, "he collects those."

"I don't think I could take Milton into the bath even now."

Helen looked at him. "You're just like Michael," she said, "all books, all sacred. How you must have been brought up."

She stopped suddenly and shouted upstairs, "We're down here." "Finally," she said to Zach, and smiled again.

Michael came down the stairs with a comic tumbling noise, entered dramatically and headed for Helen. He put his briefcase on the table among the bottles, bread, and onions and pirouetted on his heel to Zach, "Did you see the kids?"

"He's going to see them in the morning," Helen said, "and you, too, please Michael, they're asleep."

"Oh no," Michael said. "Listen, the day just expanded. Did you get a drink, Zach? Helen, you have a drink? Right, Michael will have a drink." He opened the bottle Helen handed him, poured himself a glass, and held it out in front of them. "Cheers," he said, "I'm glad we're all here."

Zach sat very still on his chair, as though retracting his presence, trying to reduce his pull as audience for the unnatural, excited patter. If he weren't there, would Michael be making these jokes of body and speech, dancing, as he now was, between English wife and American brother?

"Got a society for everything here," he was saying, "even a Wine Society. Don't have to be elected, just follow the rules."

In 1965 when Zach returned to America, Michael had gone to London, equipped himself on Carnaby Street, moved to Chelsea, to Notting Hill, following the line of sixties energy like a boy on a paper chase. Later, when the dark ages returned, the era of bespoke tailors and ventures into real estate, Michael had dipped into his American background, remembered his street slang, peppered his act with gnomic Yiddish and L.A. smartass, and advanced through an advertising career as the Real Thing. At present what was left was a fetching slaughter of idiom, miscegenation of diction, in a ragbag of vowels and regional affiliation. Nowadays, when Michael told a Jewish joke, he tended to give it the accent of Golders Green.

Yet for all Michael's noisiness, Helen upstaged him. Zach watched how she went on calmly chopping, stirring, impervious to her acrobatic courtier. Now Zach wanted Michael not to try so hard for them, now he wanted Helen to respond to his brother. Helen seemed to only half listen, half-smiling. Unobtrusively, she moved her husband around inside the room, away from the stove, away from herself as again and again his body crept towards her, drink forward, the talk aimed at Zach, the flesh veering to Helen.

Zach watched and drank and laughed when he had to, passed things to Helen when she asked him. Then he realized he had drunk too much, that, lying low in this scenario, he had done himself in.

Heavily, he got up and made his way towards the downstairs loo. Like everything else in Helen's house, it was conquered territory, the close walls a homely green, a wooden seat on the porcelain, a Victorian wood-framed print above the basin. Over the tiny barred window above the tank, vines grew outside. Nothing in this house escaped Helen's anchoring, was that it? Even here, where Zach peed long and noisily, was an insistence on civilization of a sort. It wasn't overdecorated, it wasn't pretentious or especially pretty, but the narrow space had rhetoric, spoke of home plainness, solidity, probably as alien to Helen's nervy bluestocking upbringing as it was to Michael and Zach's. The green paint and wooden seat had clear expression: the owner's passage matters. Or perhaps it was—in its simplicity and difference from New York custom, where johns were either swathed in flowers, function-disguising, or left to fend for themselves on the premise a user gets in and gets out, thoughts elsewhere—that in England matter signifies. Drunkenly, Zach thought about this, and on that evidence guessed that Helen didn't believe very much in God.

Zach believed in God very occasionally. When Maggie had first left, Zach realized that God had been invented as a way out of the foolishness of speaking to yourself. But after the worst period, God had come to seem an embarrassment, linked in his head to his own crazed state, part of the chaos like the drinking. When that early pain subsided, God had been mercifully forgotten, like an ingratiated surgeon once the hospital stay is over. Once or twice the thing had reappeared for Zach at odd moments like these inside Michael and Helen's loo, not the creature itself, but the space for him. One day he would arrive with a baggage of terminology, his very own grammar, and Zach would know that silently he'd been hatching him all along. Their last encounter had been during the summer demoralization, when unshaven, sick, and not eating, Zach had caught sight of himself in the mirror. He'd cried out "Jesus," and eye to eye with the possibility, he'd been scared.

Zach came out of the room and met the cat in the hallway. It no longer looked offended, only wary. Zach felt guilty with cats, they had his number. Dogs were too stupid. Zach passed with dogs as a good-natured sort. This cat and he were never going to break the ice. There was no point trying.

"We're really closing in on Triumph," Michael was saying to Helen, "they're sinking fast."

"When will you know? Zach, are you ready to eat?" Helen, bending in front of the oven, looked up at him from under her heavy hair and smiled. There was a maternal quality about this, remoteness and dispassion, Michael's work no more important than Zach's hunger. Michael, cued by Helen, looked at his brother, stopped his account of the day, sided parentally, fellow host: "Take some more wine, Zach, let's eat."

They moved into a smaller room, ate off oak, raffia mats, and earthenware plates, a rich dish of beef, cream, and dill, with vegetables still bruised and stained from recent garden habitation.

"It's wonderful in London," Zach said, "how people live as though they were in the country."

"Except the garden would be bigger, and the boys could play beyond the front door, and the rates wouldn't be so high."

"Helen thinks of our moving out of London altogether," Michael said, "then we do a couple of weekends involving two four-hour drives, two four-hour drives with Mick and Willis I might add, and the subject mysteriously disappears. Anyway, I like it here. I've liked this house for six years and I'll always like it." He looked around him, caught himself, and smiled foolishly.

"It's a beautiful house," Zach said.

"Country life wouldn't suit your brother," Helen said, "except perhaps some unreachable cottage in Cornwall with the boys and me packed off all summer, Michael taking an occasional train on weekends, when the office girls let him." An anxious look went up from Michael to Zach, in case he didn't see this was Helen's joke. Even Helen, remembering the era before the reliable marital understandings, back to her first clumsy encounters with the American literalness that lurked flat-footedly among the decorative ironies, hesitated in case Zach took her remarks at face value.

"Actually, summers we stay here usually, or take a few weeks in France, where of course it rains."

"We went to the Club Med in Corsica this year," Michael said, "brought the brats to shame the singles. Not too popular."

"They were very civilized," Helen said, "they're not normally, as you will see when you meet them tomorrow."

"I believe Helen refers to the American influence," Michael said proudly. "I say, OK they're a little wild now, think of the shrink bills they save later."

"Oh, this is Mike's theory," Helen said. She got up to take their plates, refusing to hear it all again.

"We don't castrate them at four in the English fashion, and we certainly don't dump them into the abyss of class warfare and sexual depravity at public school. They go locally, and even as it is, come back with hair-raising prejudices. I want you to know I may have forfeited my American vote, but I still push the Liberal-Democrat line."

"I relied on it," Zach said.

"Last month Willis came home saying the Jews this the Jews that, I couldn't believe it. I started making speeches, threw around words like *Nazi*, *pogrom*, *Diaspora*, harangued the kid for half an hour on World War Two and Leon Uris until I realized I was scaring the shit out of him, that from now on the whole issue and mere mention of the word *Jew* is going to trigger a memory of his father's hysterics. In twenty years he'll probably have confused my position with Hitler's. And of course Mick's got his problems in that department, a little shortsighted of us to stick him with the nickname. Jagger notwithstanding, he'll have to fight the anti-Irish all his life. At least I can be grateful Willis isn't taken for a pickaninny, he would back home. Dangerous business naming kids."

"I can see that."

"But I mean," Michael went on, speaking "Briddish" and waving his wrist, "I could not bring myself to call the dear things Julian, Miles, or Sebastian. Come to that, our names . . . mine travels, but yours . . ." Michael raised his eyebrows, "positively smacks of corn pone, if not, my dear, of the Chosen Race."

"It's been assumed before."

"My brother, the wandering Jew," Michael said a little sharply.

"Zach, I've made gooseberry fool," Helen said as she came back into the room, "but you don't have to have it, there's fruit."

"No, you have to have Helen's wonderpud," Michael said. He took his wife's hand and kissed it, his perfect Delilah, shearing him of his Yankeeness, yoking him to his English life. "It's super," he said.

"Super?" Zach asked him.

"Sup-ah," Michael restated.

"Well, I thought the American thing was raw food and Perrier," Helen said.

"Does this look like a man led by the nose in culinary fashions?" Michael demanded.

"Perhaps someone who watches what he eats."

"Rebuked," Michael said. He looked down at his white-waistcoated belly and hung his head.

"Come on," Helen said, "how many fools?"

"You don't suppose we're going to fall for that one?" Michael said. He smiled childishly, proud in front of his brother, pleased how well they were shining for him, the happy couple, and proud in front of Helen because he and Zach were sitting there together, brothers.

After coffee, Zach could have said, *if* he could have said, because his thoughts fled delivery, because Michael's Society wine swirled unhappily with what Helen had given him earlier, "I'll see you two in the morning." Then he could have lain upstairs while Michael and Helen reunited: "I thought you said Zach was in trouble, he seems OK," or "What am I supposed to do with him while you're at the office tomorrow?" Something sentimental from his brother: "You're some wonderful cook, Helen, wife? lover?" Would they make love this evening, Michael recharged by Zach as family man, secretly triumphing inside Helen over Zach's divorced state, or Helen, reaching out an unanxious arm, drawing Michael back into her Englishness and his real home?

Zach sat at the table and pulled himself from these thoughts, ashamed to be speculating on their actions. About himself and Maggie after such an evening, no speculation was necessary, memory would do. In that last year, postmortem recriminations: Zach's inadequacy, their guests' impossibility, Maggie's unstemmable unhappiness. That or their fast, angry, unsynchronized sleep.

"Don't mind if I leave you, Zach," Helen said. "Michael will show you your room." Zach made a clumsy effort to rise, thanking her for dinner, too late now to offer to leave himself. He sat down again as Michael put two glasses and a bottle of cognac on the table between them.

Zach waited as Michael poured unsteadily. It was early September, the evening still close enough to make them both warm. Michael's tropical clothing looked grubby now, soft. Zach waited for the change of gear that would initiate a serious cross-questioning. But Michael surprised him:

"How do we seem to you?" he asked.

"You two? Great. Helen looks great."

"She is great," Michael said. "And work's going OK, and those kids are terrific, you'll see."

"And yet?"

"And yet," Michael said. "No 'and yet,' I just wanted to know how it seemed."

"Jesus, what an advertising man you are, Michael. You wanted to know if the picture's coming across?"

"To you, kiddo, not the average TV viewer. I wanted to know what's coming across to my super-critical, never-miss-a-trick big brother."

"I'm not watching you. Christ, Michael, I'm glad to see you."

"I don't know, I mean it's perfect, isn't it, it's what I always wanted. I feel on top of everything, Zach, yet I keep wanting to creep over the edge to see how far down it is."

"Maybe that's me, Mike. Because I say I'm down. You know you always made me some kind of hero. Maybe it scares you that I've come loose."

"That isn't it," Michael said quickly. "You were always loose and heading for the sidewalk. No one would ever take your footing for a sure thing, that's always been your trip."

"Michael, 'stateside' we haven't used the word 'trip' . . ."

"I mean it, 'trip,' your passage—my wandering WASP," Michael said. "I'm not surprised you're here, and as for you and Maggie, that was just more adventure: 'I'm Maggie, fly me,' so she turned out to be a DC 10, who's surprised?"

"You're so loyal," Zach said. "You never liked Maggie."

"Sure I did. I like girls like Maggie, I just never wanted my brother to marry one. No look, I was sorry about you and her. Of course I'm sorry, I know it's been hell. Listen, I hate separations, any kind. When I was a kid in biology class, I used to cry watching those films of cells dividing."

Michael refilled their glasses. "I don't know, is this it?" he said.

"Is what it?"

"I don't know, nothing's wrong. Does that mean that's it?"

"What are you trying to do, cheer me up, tell me that being happy doesn't make you happy?"

"Is that what I'm saying?"

"Sounds like it."

They sat for a while without talking. Then Zach said, "What is it Michael, you want to come with me? You want a little bachelor vacation? Maybe you've been in advertising too long."

"What does that mean?"

"That you don't trust what you see."

"You mean I don't know Helen's quality?"

"But you do, don't you?"

"It's nothing to do with Helen, I just feel . . ."

"What?"

"I don't know."

"Jesus, Michael."

"I just feel kind of nervous," Michael shifted in his seat. "No, that's not it—I don't know, I just feel like I bought something and now I've got it and I like it. I don't know, maybe I just feel my money's gone and I can't spend it again."

"That's pathetic."

"Yeah, so it can't be that, right? OK, Zach, I just want your approval and I'm glad to have it and forget it now. Now make me feel really good, tell me how fucking miserable you are."

They waited a while, trying to sober up to the conversation.

"For three years," Zach said, "and I've come here to lose it."

They were both having trouble, Zach started again.

"No, not lose it, listen to it."

"What is *it?*" Zach's catechism, Michael liked it, he'd forgotten.

"It's made me come back, I'm not sure to what or why."

44

"You mean England?"

"No, but something that may be here."

"What?" Michael's face dropped thirty years. This was Zach's under-the-tent ghost story, Michael was hanging on.

"But you know what?"

"What?"

"I have no idea what."

Michael pulled back, someone given a dud punch line. But Zach's expression hadn't changed.

"What kind of thing?" Michael said. "You mean about you?"

"No."

"About life?"

"Closer."

"Is it bigger than a bread box?"

They drank again and sat, neither knowing how long these waits were, the time alcohol-expanded.

"Do you tell Helen about these things, Michael?"

"What things? About you?"

"No, about this feeling you've got about having spent your money and being nervous about being happy."

"Christ, I can't follow this, I'm still trying to guess what's in the bread box. Yeah, I've talked to her."

"And?"

"She says 'Why do Americans think all the time about happiness?' "

"Tell her it's in our Constitution."

"Actually, she was pretty good; she told me a story about herself in Paris."

By alcoholic wiring they were connecting.

"It was from before we got married. I was half the time in L.A., you remember, twelve, thirteen years ago. Helen was writing then, you remember she wrote poems. She quit her job in publishing, hardly publishing, more like antique-cataloguing with pictures. Anyway, she had enough money to be away from things for about a year. She says she spent every morning in her hotel in Paris too frightened to go out, too scared by whatever was going on with her to sit still and write. She had to make herself write, then in the afternoon she had to make herself go out. I mean, here was Paris. She'd saved all this money to get there, time was short. She knew some people in Montparnasse and one evening she walked all the way across Paris, like a heavy-duty march, she says, pushing herself each step, fighting God knows what, agoraphobia, xenophobia. After about an hour and a half she arrives at the Bar Select, stops, panics, big decision. Here it is. She wonders whether to go on, but she forces herself to sit down at the bar six-thirty one evening, a nice, shy, beautiful foreign girl alone in Paris. It takes all her nerve to order her drink and sit there staring straight ahead, keeping cool. You know Helen attracts attention."

"Sure," Zach said.

"She said it was nerves of steel stuff, like holding your hand in a flame. Anyway, Helen says she suddenly got this huge sense of how totally batty the whole thing was. All this suffering, every morning and every afternoon, when ten years before if she could have invented for herself an image of what she most wanted in the world, it would have been that—what she had then—being a poet, alone, young and beautiful and free, writing in Paris in the mornings, walking through Paris in the afternoons, sitting in the evening in Hemingway's Bar Select before having dinner with friends in Montparnasse. Not a tourist, but living there, having it for real. And here she was, experiencing all this as though there was something in it that was going to do her in. Helen says she received all this as some lesson about our inadequacy to our dreams, as a joke, as a warning to malcontents: Woe to him who gets to live out his own definition of happiness. Anyway, according to Helen, this was a huge notion and made her laugh out loud in front of everybody at the bar."

"And then she came to love Paris?"

"Not quite, there's a big gap between revelation and application. Also, her morality tale had another morality tale inside, because, she says, as soon as she let go like this and realized how lucky she was, suffering though she was, to be there, this figure appeared. In her fuzz, you know the way you do with famous people, you forget you recognize them because they're famous, you make some sign of hello until you remember who they are. Helen nodded to this famous face and the famous face nodded back and then she realized it was that big French movie star from the sixties— I can't remember the name. Anyway, he saunters towards her, his hand tapping his hat. This is my day, she thinks, first the revelation, now him. But as he passes her table suddenly he keels over and falls down dead drunk in front of her, unshaven and dead drunk. The famous star was a bum."

"You mean it was a bum?"

"No, it was a famous star. You know that child actor, the one who got beaten up in that film about the little boy. Then he had a film every few years. You know him."

"So where's the moral?"

"I don't know, this child star, growing up famous. He should have been happy, too, but he was a bum at thirty. To Helen the whole thing connected."

"And then what happened?"

"She got up, paid the bill, and went to dinner."

"I don't get it."

"Well, you get to pick: either I must be a fool if I'm not happy with this, or just woe to him that gets to live his definition of happiness," Michael said again.

"And this is your definition of happiness?"

"It's pretty close. Yeah, Helen, Mick, Willis, the house, the job, the life."

"But?"

"I don't know what the *but* is like you don't know what's in the bread box."

"It's the family curse," Zach said heavily.

"You think so?"

"Well, you, me, Dinah, how come nobody lives at home?"

"What do you mean, nobody? I'm at home, this is it, you're in it now."

"And the *but* tells me you're not convinced."

There was another five minutes before either of them spoke.

"You always drink like this?" Michael asked Zach.

"Yeah. You?"

"Yeah. Let's put you to bed."

They got up unsteadily. Michael put away the cognac, and with a little concentration, aligned his chair against the table. Zach copied him. Then with one arm over his brother's back, Michael pushed them both towards the stairs, reaching to turn out the lights as they went.

"Perrier, Helen says!" Michael said to Zach.

They parted on the second landing.

"In there," said Michael. "If you need anything you're on your own. Bathroom's upstairs. The kids are upstairs. Try not to shout in your sleep."

Zach woke to the sound of a sharp singsong voice crying "Uncle." It pitched high through the fog of the previous night's drinking, dispersing his dreams so they rolled away like marbles. He tried to pursue them as they slid down cracks, multicolored, cheap, fleeting. Something from Maggie in those dreams, her power over him. A late echo now as he woke, the smile, and a phrase of hers, from before the time they did each other harm. How did she speak to him? Without defenses. What was it she said?

"Uncle. Uncle." The voice pulled at him once more.

The name of a place, and Maggie's brother in the dream, only years younger. When Tom was sixteen. The visit to Edgartown, polished hotel floors, cast-iron bed, flowers in the room overpowered by the smell of the sea. Maggie unpacking there and Tom impatient for them to come onto the boat. Skipper for someone for the season. Maggie's idea to spend the weekend.

Zach looked for a moment at Tom's impatient face, then saw Mick standing above him, watching him wake.

"Uncle," Mick said. He smiled and waited, uncertain of the effect of the word.

Zach tried to wake up now, pulling himself from the child's scrutiny: this uncle with red eyes and sour breath, denting deep into the child's attention.

Mick stood patiently, giving Zach time to focus. The boy had Helen's eyes and translucent skin.

"You are my uncle," Mick said formally.

"Hello, Mick."

"Here's Willis." Mick stood out of the way and pushed the smaller boy towards him. Willis looked at his own shoes, not interested in this uncle, or shy.

"Willis."

Willis gave Zach a slightly jaded look, a small version of his hungover dad. Zach laughed. "What time is it, fellas?"

"Who's fellas?"

"What time, chaps?" Zach sat up. He was in a large room with pine cupboards and flowered paper. Corners of a white-lacquered sill emerged from heavy curtains. He pointed. "Is it late? Let's have a look."

Mick's small, grubby hand tugged at the chintz and the room flooded theatrically with light. "It's late," Willis said, "after ten."

Willis stood rocking on his feet, staring in disapproval.

"Come on," Mick said finally. He gave Zach a conspiratorial wave and pushed the younger boy ahead of him through the door.

Zach sank down and shut his eyes against the sun. Tom again, who took his life at twenty-six. Maggie said it was because no one made him welcome in the world. They'd shut the doors like bad hosts after Tom had his breakdown. Maggie blamed herself, but Zach knew it wasn't that. Tom had told him. Too much death for Tom. First the parents, and a year later Alison. Alison went so slowly her dying adhered to him. He couldn't shake it, not even when he came apart, throwing himself recklessly downward like a dog getting rid of a smell. It had wrapped him and taken him. Tom told Zach that at the hospital. Later, when he was out, working, new job, new town, new girl, they all figured he was OK. It had been a surprise.

Some people thought Tom loved Alison too much, beyond what is reasonable and safe. Zach tried to imagine loving a woman to the point of exit. He could have loved Maggie that way, but it was she who had stopped him. Perhaps you have to love yourself excessively to be able to take it from somebody else. Had Zach ever been loved like that? What did it feel like? Like a bad contract. His mother, that was the only one. A one-sided deal: sit still and let me love you. By thirteen, he could barely breathe. And then Michael not getting his, because Zach had it all. Dinah, much later, what had she got? Teen-age fights, sexual jealousy. Over Zach, Maggie said. Maggie and his mother never fought, far too dangerous, they never even approached from the corners. Therefore, Maggie can see Zach's mother even now, when Zach can't and Michael and Dinah don't. Maggie reproaches Zach with his mother's loneliness. That's because she doesn't see the size of the club the lady aims at her baby seal.

*   *   *

Motion sickness as Zach rose from bed, alcohol still in his exhalations. Helen had put a towel outside his door with a note that bid him good morning. He made his way to the upstairs bathroom, wearing his trousers in case she back-tracked through the house. Women's voices downstairs, sunlight on the landings. Steam rose onto the mirror and windowpanes as Zach ran his bath. A dark red room, pretty again, but not so much fun as his hotel bathroom, where they gave you gifts every morning, cellophane-wrapped razor, new soap, handy little pieces of quilted paper with pictures and instructions: "shoe-wiper," "please use for lipstick." Each morning a new cover for the toothbrush mug, clean towels with the hotel's name cut in fabric, white, stiff. If you were so inclined you could take all this by way of sou-venirs. Maggie liked to steal ashtrays, giant ones, carried them under her jackets, exiting deadpan from elegant restau-rants, while Zach hung back and paid extra to the waiters.

Nothing wrapped or shining here. Zach opened their cabinet, shaved himself with Michael's razor, used some-one's toothbrush, telling himself to move his kit in later so they would not guess and be shocked. When he was living with Maggie, anyone opening their bathroom cabinet could have seen something was amiss. Maggie's prescriptions for health and happiness: pills for sleeping, for speeding, for dieting, for calming down, unbelievable quantities of makeup.

The way bathrooms throw these things together, Zach threw them together too, the pills and the beauty aids: just Maggie's professional equipment. Her wild swings: days she bounded in jeans and sneakers like someone looking for a street game, evenings dragged through as though she'd done both performances of *The Oresteia*. The day-to-day grief she'd been capable of, and despair. Her despair, though, like his of recent months, was something you could be talked out of. Not that peaceful resolution of Tom's. Mood swings, mixed and adulterated by Maggie's confused self-scrutiny and oddball feminism, her insistence on being "real" at home. The world got the adman's dream of chic and cheer, pressed clothes, plucked brows; Zach got the furrows and frayed bathrobe, Maggie scowling at base camp, the real thing.

At home, the character actress; at work, she took the roles she was given pretty unfussily for someone so touchy about stereotyping, so up in the terminology of authenticity. The odd thing was the agencies more or less had Maggie's number. They caught the innocence, turned it into foolishness, starring her in tales of humiliation: the hopeless housewife, the products always introduced by the brighter neighbor while Maggie coped with grief and disappointment in her family: boys and men inadequately fed, scratched by detergents, ready to leave because of the toothpaste.

Not just this paying work, she'd also done out-of-town runs, culture brought to the mountains, Radio Free Suburbia. Her wanting to be an actress was strange in itself given her terror: her natural camera smile, a kind of smirk, a small offer of goodwill sabotaged by a muscle spasm of defense that pulled her mouth sideways in front of the lens. Calming exercises gave her a steadier expression, but too long a close-up and her smile would slide into car sickness.

That terror, of course, she used; Maggie could speak for hours about nerves, bottom points, black wells. Acting theory, Zach had had up to here, it had even supplied the terminology of their separation. "You have to do the thing you are afraid of, sooner or later," Maggie had said.

"Why?" Zach asked, at first simply curious, later, pleading.

"Because unless you get it first, it just sits there, poisoning everything." She was afraid to go it alone, which was why, she said, Zach had to leave.

It was as though Maggie had become less when she began to live with Zach, had lost her balance. Yet when he had first known her, it was her composure and containment that had attracted him. He used to visit her after work, climbing the four flights of her Village brownstone like some religious devotee ascending to peace and light. And she had always meant peace and light to him, stillness, radiance, welcome.

He imagined marriage to her like that, his nightly return to her nightly welcome; greeted, wanted, embraced in the overflow of her contentment, made to feel his existence gave joy to hers. But it hadn't turned out that way. His existence had removed her defenses, made her dependent and unsure, as though her first composure had been acting only, which, Zach was sure, it had not.

But how painfully different were those first welcomes from the last ones, when Maggie would pretend to ignore him, editing out the sounds of his entrances, growing visibly tenser as he removed his coat, lay down his work, tried to come inside, still not understanding, but like some poor untrainable beast seeking her out, willing the embrace that would end the nightmare of their coming apart. He had never understood, not her unhappiness nor her change towards him.

"Lovely to see you," Helen's voice. Zach, out of the bathroom, peered, barefoot, betrousered, over the stairs down to the hall landing. Two women embraced, dark, slender, happy.

"Morning." She looked up and waved.

"Is that Zach?" Helen.

"Morning."

"I'm off."

"I'm coming down."

"This is Anne; Michael's brother, Zach."

"Welcome," a welcoming smile. "I'm off."

Gone. Shirt and shoes. Down to Helen.

Waiting for the uptown express last year, the train late, three middle-aged black women stood near him, howling down their men. The furies reciting: treachery, drink; choral voices. Then, more in sorrow, how it is: men. The tallest of them, owner of the fur-imitating hat, her lips outlined, two shades of red, took the lead. Who her man was. She liked her story the more she told it: For twenty years, other women, out all night, a weak man, a bad man. And now this morning she'd told him: now it's enough, out and stay out. "Because," she said, smiling, knowing, "life too sweet— life too sweet to waste on Washington."

Anne was going to come to dinner. Helen thought Zach might like her. Michael said Helen was crazy. They had taken him to the theater and out among the married couples, and gradually understood that he seriously meant to be in London. They thought he would need more than themselves if he was going to stay. Still, Michael had put up a strange fight when Anne was suggested:

"Anne and Zach." Michael had laughed.

"What's funny?"

"Nothing funny, just Helen's basket case, not a marble left. A walking disaster, alcoholic, manic-depressive, accident prone, kleptomaniac, just what you need right now."

"Shut up, Michael," Helen said. "I hate it when you're cruel."

"I'm trying not to be cruel to Zach. She takes things and never returns them, she owes us money, she stayed here a week and sleepwalked every night, she drank two bottles of scotch."

"Stop it, Michael." Helen got up and left the room.

"Who is she?" Zach asked him.

"Some old friend of Helen's. I wouldn't get near that one in a million years."

"You speak with feeling."

"What, me, are you serious? You know I don't fool around. Just trust me on this, she's got some record."

"This is all very enticing. Who is she? What does she do?"

"She drinks, she cries."

"A real doll. For a living, Michael, what does she do for a living?"

"A fat zero. Lives off the kindness of people like Helen."

"Anne what?"

"Depends who she's married to. Look, she's some old friend of Helen's, from Paris. She used to paint or make pots or something. She married some pansy Brit, went to Africa, someplace melodramatic, came back, divorced, broke up some perfectly nice marriage, married, divorced, started drinking, went through a lot of money. I don't know, Helen told me the story once. I was touched, we had her here. She nearly did us in. I don't like her."

"No!"

"I don't trust her. She's not honest. I don't like her in the house."

"Jesus, Michael."

"Well, I'm telling you. She's pretty special."

"What do you mean, she's a kleptomaniac?"

"She takes things home with her. Helen pretends they're gifts."

"Maybe they are gifts."

"Willis's bear?"

"Maybe Willis gave it to her."

"Maybe he did. Listen, Zach, far be it from me to dictate who you can see, or who Helen can have to dinner. We'll have her. Just watch your wallet, that's all."

Zach wore the English suit he had bought on Jermyn Street. Michael wore tropical gear from which he seemed to bulge, white-shirted, like the contents of a manila envelope. Helen wore a cowl-necked teal wool dress and gold, spotted scarf. Anne sat among them in a silk dress with shoulder pads, wearing high, shiny shoes and a demure smile. Two small seams had sprung open along the forearms. Everyone had dressed for a different play.

Looking at her, Zach was reminded vaguely of women's war work, of soldiering on alone in a manless place. The vampishness seemed harnessed, a kind of munitions factory bravado, cheerful, but with the heart not quite in it. She smiled perhaps too often, ready to be helpful, help things go, and yet she remained separate from them, something in her body suggesting her irony, a defense acknowledging she was not quite in step. Who were they to make her feel it so hard?

It was one of Michael's bad nights. By now Zach had seen a few, no longer hidden by Michael's obligation as host. Tonight he seemed jumpy, his jokes running sharp and the rhythm off. Helen appeared to ignore him, automatically letting her placidity line and coat the edges where Michael's mood threatened to show. Tensely, Michael removed pieces of cork from a misopened bottle. Helen picked up his erratic chatter and recoded it into her own soothing, welcoming hum. And she slowed her movements against the staccato of his, exaggerated the stirring of soup, concentrated her tasting. Zach held himself out of the performance, waiting for Michael to slow down, for Helen to give up her attempted control of the evening. Once, twice, Anne crossed her legs and Zach listened to the slither of nylon, assessed her under the cover of marital theatrics, the uncomfortable Mike-Helen mime he thought both of them watched with as little happiness as the audience at an amateur evening (elbows and Bartok) of contemporary dance.

In the silence they were allied. When they began to speak they would go to separate corners. Watching Michael as he stirred cream into his soup, backward and around, making patterns, Zach surrendered to the necessity of speech when Anne began.

"Helen says you are going to be in England a few months. You'll have to stay forever if you stay that long. But perhaps you'll get bored after a couple of weeks. London is no place for long visits."

"This may be true," Michael said sourly, "Zach's already done Bond Street, bought a pair of shoes, been to the RSC, time to think of moving on." Michael returned to his soup mournfully. "Any more of this?" he asked Helen.

"Where will you go?" Anne asked him.

"Why is everyone telling Zach to leave?" Helen said. "Why shouldn't he stay?"

"Because he'll never be English," Anne said seriously, "and in the end England is a bad place for tourists."

"How do you know so much about Zach?" Michael challenged her.

"You could be right," Zach said. He was eager to get in before Helen started soothing feathers. "So how would I become British? How would I get to stay?"

"You gotta pass a medical, make sure there's no alien blood, gotta do speech therapy . . ."

"Stop, Michael," Helen said. "Let Anne say."

"You do have to learn the language," Anne said seriously, "and with absolute precision you have to learn the codes, the way soldiers have to know how to take their weapons apart. You have to have perfect camouflage. The enemy has a million ways of finding you out."

"What enemy?" Zach said. "What about Michael?" he asked unwisely. Anne, graciously, not unnoticeably, declined to answer.

"Michael has decided to do without camouflage," Helen said for her, "and though he sticks out like a sore thumb, it doesn't bother him. But it might bother someone else."

"What sore thumb? Are you kidding? You know how I'd come across if I started talking like you two? Anyway, what is this shit, Anne? I'm accepted. Dammit, I've lived here twenty years, are you telling me *now* I don't belong?"

"I notice you become exaggeratedly American under attack," Zach said to him.

"We protect you," Helen said, "your family. Out in the big world you'd be ripped to shreds."

"You two make London sound pretty dangerous," Zach said.

"You make it sound like a cockney musical starring Julie

Andrews. This is a metropolis, ladies. We've got every nationality in the world out there walking the streets without fear for life or dignity. You girls ought to get out of the house more."

"It's true," Anne said to Zach. "No place to visit."

"Cut it, Anne," Michael said angrily. "Look, Zach's just got here. He wants a little shelter. Let's not all tell him the ceiling leaks—OK?"

"OK," Anne said cheerfully. She'd dented the evening, or Michael. Zach saw how she liked it. Again he wondered about those two. Evidently there was a line between them, in Michael's case, frayed wiring.

Several times during the evening they fell back into safe positions: Helen and Anne talking about mutual friends, Michael acting preoccupied host, Zach the courteous foreigner. The women's talk started and faltered, getting to the point where privacy was needed and there stopping. Michael frequently stopped them, orchestrating their meal, collecting their plates, bumping against the table like a man with more important things on his mind. No cognac this evening, not much display of domestic bliss.

"Got a train to catch?" Zach asked him, when Helen went up to check on the boys.

Michael stopped, looked at his watch and sat down.

"Perhaps I should get a cab," Anne offered.

"It's eleven," Michael said flatly.

"Does that mean it's only eleven, or eleven already?" Anne asked him.

"It's only eleven," Zach said calmly.

"I'll wait for Helen, then I'll go."

"I'll take you back," Zach said. Michael raised his brows.

"Thanks, but it's a long way. If you take me back you won't be back yourself for a couple of hours."

"That's fine with me," Zach said, "I've nothing on to-morrow." He looked at Michael, this remark was meant to excuse his brother's rudeness. Or cue him.

"Well, I have," Michael said, cued to rudeness.

"We get the picture," Zach said. "You're making things horribly clear." Both Anne and Zach laughed at him.

"Look, you people stay. Have a drink. I may go up, but Helen's here, and you two are here. What's the problem?"

"No problem," Zach said indulgently, and to Anne, "I'll take you back."

"Well, you two work it out," Michael said. "Forgive me for abandoning you." He moved towards the door. With his formality returned to him, he looked a little sheepish. He hovered, waiting apparently for some absolution.

"It's been lovely," Anne said to him. "Good to see you."

Michael gave a short nod, looked at his brother.

"Sweet dreams," Zach said.

Michael hesitated, waiting for some further good-night, then retreated upstairs.

"I won't wait for Helen," Anne said, "I'll get a cab. It's easier, truly, I'm miles from Hampstead. But thank you."

"I'm not tired," Zach said, "so unless you really want to be alone crossing London . . ."

"You mean crying in the back of the cab?"

"I mean . . ."

63

"Don't be silly," she said. "I'm fine. And you're fine."
She touched his arm lightly and turned towards the stairs.
Halfway up she paused. "Are you coming to the door?"

"I'm coming to wherever you live."

"All right," Anne said, "but not tonight."

"When?" Zach asked rather gravely.

"Would Friday do?"

"Friday. Where do I go?"

She gave him the address. "Can you remember that? But
Helen has it."

Zach repeated the address, again gravely.

Anne laughed, "It sounds such a slum in an American
accent."

"Anne," Zach said. She had her hand on the door, opening it slowly. "Let me come with you. I'll take you home
and bring the cab back. It's just another way to see London."

"You're awfully stubborn," she said.

They walked down the sloping street, towards the main
road. Zach wanted to speak, pull his weight inside the
peculiar situation, make up for his insistence, explain it as
apology for their evening, but he felt an odd caution with
her, as though he wanted only to tell the truth, to start from
scratch, all new. He wanted her approval, to win her without
flirting. His uncarelessness surprised him. He looked at her
as they walked and when she looked back at him, found
himself asking her, inanely, if she were cold.

"It isn't cold," she said.

"I used to live around here," she said, "a few streets away
during one terrible winter. It was a basement flat on the

hill where a big psychiatric center is. I used to watch the ankles of what I imagined were all the depressives in London on their way toward the center. It felt like the basin for all the misery in the world, that place that winter. Winter is no fun in London."

The slow noise of a diesel crept behind them. Zach stepped out in the road and waved the driver down.

"I saw you," he said irritably.

"Good." Zach got in. Anne stayed on the pavement giving directions. Zach remembered now you did your business with cabbies on the street. Zach recalled a scene in New York, the time an English visitor had gotten out of a taxi to pay the driver, how the driver had thought he was being robbed. Worst of all, once matters were explained, the Englishman, broad-grinning, pink, and benign, had rewarded the driver with a dime, with predictable verbal consequences.

"Aggressive, aren't they?" he had said, still smiling, after the driver tried to run him down. The man had been pleased by the colorful encounter, Zach embarrassed. He wondered now vaguely whether Anne would be, here, by him. Gaucheness would get in the way of what he wanted from her. What did he want from her? The not-so-perfect stranger. Zach seemed strange to himself. To be honest with her. No secrets, no sham. As though for the first time. And what good did he think that would do? Still, he wanted that, the foreign experience.

"I feel I ought to apologize for Michael," Zach said. But he meant himself.

"Don't," Anne said. "It couldn't matter less.'"

"You didn't say why you were going to be here so long," she said. "Don't you have work?"

"At the moment, no work," Zach said. "No reason to be in New York. So I'm here."

"With what reason, though, here?"

"No reason."

"Like me," Anne said.

"But you have work." He paused. Michael had said not. "Or family?"

"I'm divorced," Anne said simply. "No children. I do some jewelry designing. Not very energetically."

She didn't apologize, yet she seemed to anticipate some judgment.

"You could live, then, somewhere else?" Zach asked her.

"I used to. I came back. Back is where you come when you run out of reasons to be away."

"Guaranteed?"

"Guaranteed. You'll go home." She looked at him, directly, almost in challenge, till she caught herself and smiled.

"It doesn't feel like leaving home, being here," Zach said seriously. "More like trying to find it."

She looked at him. "Now that's a peculiar thing for a grown man to say."

"Yes," Zach admitted.

"And you're not really a hippie."

"I wouldn't say it to everyone," Zach said. That sounded flirtatious. Anne made light of it. "It's only because you're in transit you feel so free to speak your mind."

"In a moving vehicle," he said. "Then we could stop. Speak in a stationary manner."

"Boastfully, evasively," Anne said, "that manner? How people hide who can't run. How do you propose we stop," she asked, "in the middle of nowhere, in the middle of London?"

"We could have a drink," Zach said.

Anne looked at him warily. "This is London after midnight," she said. "Cinderella town."

"Not so," Zach said, gaily now. He took her hand. "I know just the place. Brown's," he shouted at the driver, "Albemarle Street."

"It certainly doesn't sound like London when you pronounce it, I must say."

Zach squeezed her hand.

"Don't expect too much," she said.

"Oh, I do."

"I mean at Brown's."

"I know," Zach said.

Propped up at the bar, Anne came to life. It seemed to Zach that even her dress changed character, no longer diffident, rather ostentatiously sexy. She led with her shoulders as she talked, shifted on the stool. I am alive, the body said now, I am alive. And she laughed. Not loudly, but all alone in that abandoned hotel room, laughing at him and at where she was. Her laughter like her body challenging him, letting him in on the joke, which was partly himself. But she was suddenly happy.

They were alone. The group of Northern businessmen that had been noisily drinking when they arrived had departed quietly, dark suits pulling. It seemed to Zach, watching them, that unhappiness had descended on them in the hotel hallway where they waited for cabs. Their day was over, not prolongable forever, a less elegant hotel night upon them. Frightened perhaps, off to sleep alone, far from home, another day of push and smile tomorrow. Zach caught himself as he sent them to their doom, wondering how he came to project such dread onto other people's lives. He laughed at himself and his own dread, relieved in this hotel-pocket darkness with this woman, this strange woman who was making an honest man of him. The alcoholic, kleptomaniac, what else had Michael said? Very good, Zach. Way to your brother's heart. The thing is, he didn't believe Michael for one moment. And what is it you want from her? Is it the whiff of pain, my friend? That companionship. You who wanted the simple life. But it begins to feel simple. Rules of the picaresque adventure. Rule one: The hero is an idiot.

He watched Anne getting drunk, and how her body unloosened.

"More drink," Zach said. He looked around for the bartender, who, standing at a discreet distance from all this blossoming, now reappeared.

"Two doubles," Zach said.

"Whiskey, sir, or cognac?"

"Oh dear, have we been mixing them, Anne?"

"Cognac, please," she said.

The bartender poured, seemed to indicate some judgment withheld, yet offered no hospitality by manner, and no forgiveness. When he had served them, once again he disappeared.

"I'd feel guiltier if the doubles weren't half the size of American singles," Zach said.

"Feel guilty," Anne said, "they'll be doubly expensive." But their guilt had nothing to do with these things.

"Whatever the cost," Zach said grandly, "to see you happy."

"Happy?" Anne said. "Drunk."

"Is it the same?"

"Yes," Anne said.

"Then I hope you do this often," Zach said. It was wrongly said.

"Often drink in bars? No. Do I often drink? Yes, indeed."

"Alone?" Zach asked.

"Is that some American medical definition?"

"You're different now." He touched her, to show how he didn't exclude her, but sought to befriend her, address an ally.

"Not different," Anne said, "just released." She steered away from him. She attempted Southern Baptist speech, "released from the prison of mah soul."

"Yes?" Zach asked her.

"I'm afraid so," she said looking at him. This naïveté excluded her, his American friendliness. "Well, I'd take up whirling like the dervishes," she said, "but my friends would never speak to me. Not done, you know. No joy without evidence of chemical interference permitted. The world of the spirit not permitted. Or not," she intoned, "for people like one. However, perhaps I'll whirl with you, you're new, you don't know the ropes, don't know yet what's allowed and what's not. This, for example, getting drunk in a tourist bar is not allowed."

"We'll go dancing," Zach said. "Would you like that?" This was bluff. Zach's dignity shriveled on the dance floor, particularly after Maggie, who'd refused to be seen with him there. "Dead man's hips," she'd said.

"That is not the whirling I need," Anne said, wearily, as though finding herself once more alone. "You can't dance in London, anyway," she told him, "not after the age of sixteen, except at some charity function where they do the twist, self-parodying, you know, the my-wife-brought-me look. If you want to see that, or middle-aged humiliation—clenched paunches dancing with terrified debutantes—we can go to Annabel's, but we'll have to find a member. When I tell you you won't stay it's because life comes to an end here. After twenty it's meant all to be over, you get married, you have children, you wear a headscarf, you're not meant to be left to fend for yourself looking for a place to dance, drinking in bars. It's not on the program, and therefore doesn't really happen."

"And does that mean you only get to exercise your soul when some visiting foreigner lures you ignorantly into a place like this, the place and the person not scripted, likewise not really happening?"

"My dear," she answered him, "I get drunk all the time, socially correctly at dinner parties and Sunday lunches, and not so socially correctly at other times and in many other places. I am *amazed* [she leaned hard on the word] that Michael hasn't told you."

Zach turned away and held their glasses up to the bartender. "How long will he let us stay here?"

"About two, I would say, is the limit. It must be that now."

"Nearly," Zach said. "Last ones," he told the bartender. The drinks came this time with the bill. They'd spent twenty pounds in less than two hours.

"It costs a great deal to exercise the soul," Anne said, "I'm very sorry."

"It's nothing," Zach said. "And besides, there are cheaper ways."

Anne looked at him. "I'm not sure I'm ready for all this."

"All what?"

"For a person who is free."

"Lady," Zach said smiling, "have you got the wrong number."

"I don't think so," Anne said.

Zach bent his head to her hand, but she pulled away.

"You're not to kiss my hand," she said to him. "I'm a terrible person."

He looked at her.

"Take my word for it," Anne said.

She said this seriously, and he heard in that the adult knowledge, shame. Again he felt the connection, wished to offer absolution, felt his helplessness. And then the femme fatale tried to descend her stool, suddenly a little girl in costume. Zach helped her down, tried not to mock her movements in any way, had in any case to concentrate on his own. He felt tenderness then and, recognizing that, caution: she was not a child. Or perhaps, he was not much of a parent. He could not guarantee any of the compassion he felt. Could not. Experience told him. There is no first time again. In a flash he saw to the end of this, its barren conclusion. Despairing that there was no meaning to desire when you knew the ending of it, the loss that must ensue; no meaning to compassion when you could not guarantee it.

"Good night, sir, madam."

The voice, innocent of malice, yet the scorn came across. Or Zach's guilt, his shame, so close to hand. Right on tap.

"Thank you," Zach called back. He refused the correction. Perhaps it doesn't last, he told himself. But it can be repeated. With luck. And by repetition proceeds where? Karen and Maggie. No, he said now. No. The past is not the future. The past cannot always, always win.

Zach woke, and knowing where he was, was childishly happy. It seemed to him immediately that something significant had occurred, dividing today from yesterday. That everything was different. How had it happened? He had meant to deposit the girl safely home, impress her with his seriousness, his refusal to impose. She had convinced him it was not an imposition, that was how. Someone had said the magic words and the duck had fallen from the sky, blue bird of happiness whose feathers still wafted overhead this gray-coated London morning. What words? A mutual confession of fear and frailty, an understanding come to inside the rumble of drink, din of false intimacy, all the night's misjudged signals of desire and promise. But then something had been delivered and heard; something accurately aimed, had gone home, had worked like children's magic, like a gift of seven-league boots, to let them through and across the vast distances between them.

She had touched him last night, using drink, parodying

her own clumsiness to disguise what she nevertheless directed him to see/hear: a line on which tenderness had been hooked, a small fragile, connecting question. For one moment her eyes—hunted, insolent—seemed to be lit by something that signaled briefly, then buried itself opaque once more. But he had seen it. He remembered it now, and the quiver at the corner of her mouth. A pulse at her throat had caught him, its current low and regular like wiring in a field, warming her body, charging her skin with life. Skin was alive. How long had he forgotten that? His hand had shaped her easily, ecstatically, in broad and perfect arabesques, and she had held him as though she might fall far and forever away.

The moment was gone, remembered only, a grace given. No, not so passively surrendered. Breathing in, he knew again that this mattered. More than sensation. To live was to receive such moments; wisdom, to proceed in such a way that the moments would find you out, ready, accepting. Accepting, too, that they can bear no weight. That was the hard part, to open your hand and agree to let them go. And then between such moments nothing, nothing that mattered. Really, no meaning to be construed from all the surrounding darkness in which the points of light arrived, as haphazardly, and unprovoked it seemed, as they went. Right now Zach felt it possible to abandon his argument with the darkness, stop shaking it, hoping to turn it into light, or lights: these moments that came, would come again. No, the wisdom was only the waiting.

Zach got up, sat on the edge of the bed and looked at

her across the hallway. She was sitting on the arm of a white chair, her head turned away from him as she smoked a cigarette inside a patch of sunlight that fell on bare feet and red silk robe. She seemed immeasurably far from him, lost to him, and so sad in her privacy that he dared not interrupt. He watched her, how her hand with the cigarette moved and left smoke tracings in the sun that came and went between the clouds. Deep in her thoughts, her head bent towards the floor, her hair hung across her cheek, she was, sitting there in her sadness, a contradiction. He could not help taking remote, formal pleasure in her loveliness, despite the bleakness inside.

Watching her now, he remembered last night how she moved, vaunting her freedom, speaking so earnestly, then frivolously, mixing clues so that your head would spin and you would thrash with her, not guess that at her center was the creature he now saw, so still, so anchored by sadness. He thought he had only to accept this being, had only to reach inside all that splash and movement, glitter and noise, to stop her spinning, let her rest, let her be, this still, sad, self.

He had only to cross to where she was, touch and free her. And then, as suddenly, Zach saw again beyond this desire, an image of the barren, futile end of it. Wanting seemed all. Taking, having, would end it. But already it was too late because he did want her. He had lost his freedom.

Now something Anne had said last night, or Maggie: Life is so disappointing.

"Anne." Her back stiffened slightly, and she turned.

"Anne." He walked towards her. She looked at him formally. "Good morning," she said and not quite said, We each have our lives.

"Good morning," Zach said, and would have said, We have only our lives. Or perhaps, We have all our lives.

Zach walked into Michael's kitchen and too late remembered the promised outing. Mick and Willis sat at the table, staring morosely as he entered the room, two uneaten sandwiches on plates in front of them.

"Hello there," Helen's neutral greeting came from the garden.

"Hi." Zach looked at Mick sideways, trying to register the degree of injured pride. Willis, he noted, made an effort to ignore him.

"OK, guys," Zach said, "have a heart. Your uncle forgot. We're still going, right?"

Helen came inside, welcoming. She had weeds and clumps of earth in a wicker basket.

"OK, we're going," Zach said again, addressing her.

"Don't you want breakfast first?" she asked him.

"Breakfast!" Willis mocked him.

"Lunch, then," Helen said cheerfully.

"Nothing. Zoo time." The excuse to be away was good.

77

Mick unfroze and ran from his place at the table. "I want to have lunch with Zach. I'm not finishing."

"I'm not finishing," Willis said, getting down, making clear his determination to keep up with his brother and not enthusiasm for the expedition.

"All right, all right," Helen said.

"I'll phone for a cab," Zach said.

"No need." Now she looked shocked. "I've got the car."

"You don't want to drive us."

"Of course I do."

They sat in the car, Helen still in her gardening clothes, and moved silently through heavy Saturday traffic. Helen turned on the car radio and they listened for a while to an actress's interview. Zach thought of neither Maggie nor Anne. He was engaged fully in catching up with his present companions.

"Here we are," Helen said, pulling up at the gates of the zoo. "Have fun." Her passengers got out dutifully with an air of low anticipation. Zach tried his best paternal manner, strained for cheerfulness under the leaden English skies, caught inside the hole that ever since the divorce Saturday afternoons anywhere always were for him.

They got through the turnstile and separated from the crowds at the gate, heading vaguely in the direction of the penguin house where, as Mick told Zach, they sometimes had underwater performances, visible through a glass partition, of female swimmers with the birds. Zach doubted Mick had this quite right, but was curious how the Times Square aura would be kept from the family fare. However decently covered, the girls would look underdressed next to the penguins, kitted as these were like Las Vegas emcees. Today, however, no mermaids, only a regular civic banquet of white-fronted waddling birds, gliding and diving through the not very clean water. Mick was disappointed.

Zach, comfortable here, watched the sport of the birds as they played for the audience, watched Mick and Willis watching, remembering as a fact from his own childhood, though no longer knowing, how much they were taking in, the huge amount of life visible to children.

In New York, Zach had always felt awkward taking Karen to the zoo, ashamed of how the animals were treated, embarrassed by the unanswerable cruelty of grown-ups, the sentimental ignorance that kept animals inside the tiny Victorian cages in Central Park, moth-eaten as thrift shop furs, pacing in despair, bellowing, or sleeping, bored unto death. Even in the more humane open spaces of the Bronx Zoo, they allowed animals to suffer the refuse missiles of the vandals. People gave lit cigarettes to monkeys and empty peanut boxes to elephants; some years ago a boy had entered the zoo at night and felled three deer and two ponies with an air rifle.

Even this looking at the animals was unpleasant to Zach, seemed an invasion, a crude demonstration of power by one set of creatures over others. Zach found zoo expeditions educational but not edifying. Yet here he was, and responsible for the outing. Mick and Willis, soon bored by the penguins and seals, the animals that seemed most to enjoy the crowds, demanded something more sensational. They walked through the indoor cages where the big cats were, lying asleep in unbreathable fumes of raw meat and urine. Zach held his breath too long and came out choking.

Mick and Willis leaned against a railing and said nothing, waiting for Zach to resume the party. Embarrassed by the small conflict of wills and their sense of imposition on him, and worse, their unasked part inside a family arrangement, they stood awkwardly, too politely, waiting. Willis hardly bothered to disguise his scorn, seemed most aware of the fraudulence of the occasion. He'd never accepted the erratically delivered bits of avuncular business, nor the ritual greetings and running gags that Zach offered with decreasing faith in his own credibility. Nor was the child, it seemed to Zach, willing as Mick was to forgive his uncle's halfheartedness. Zach detected in his small nephew an impressive tough-mindedness with regard to their relationship, Willis's challenge to him from the height of four feet to "put up or shut up." With Mick, however, there was something else, leaning into Zach and offering love, and demonstrating to him his own inadequacy at each of his inept, poorly disguised, refusals of friendship.

Zach bought them hot dogs and Cokes and led them to the requested boa constrictor. In the dark of the reptile house, he imagined he would be reprieved temporarily with a little time to remember his lines. As they wandered in the infrared glare from one glass case to another, Zach watched them, hoping this wasn't the sort of place they showed mealtimes. At the Children's Zoo in New York, Zach found it unbelievably grisly that they supplied the fluffy owls with mice right there in front of the children: little girls that wept over their own pink-tailed pets, little boys that would go home and torture kittens. He did not want to look at the boa constrictor or have to guess at the contents of the bulge that might be yesterday's supper. Constrictors had one big meal at a time and digested it for days. In England, surely, Zach comforted himself, they would humanely knock off the rats and bunnies first. In the wild those creatures died horribly, slowly disintegrating in digestive acids. Maybe Zach got that wrong, maybe there was some state of shock built in to keep the animals from suffering.

He remembered how he hadn't wanted Karen to know about these things. Even the Disney films he'd found rough going, with their long footage of prairie dogs dancing, then disappearing none too obscurely under the shadow of the hawk. Maggie said Karen should know early so it wouldn't be worse later; but Zach didn't believe that, thought if you could somehow get a head start before the facts came through you'd be stronger. He hadn't let Karen go to hospitals or funerals—Tom's, for instance. He believed enough reality lurked without having to court it. Now it all looked pretty stupid: all the years spent censoring Disney only to land her—helplessly—in her parents' divorce.

So he did not let Mick get too close to him. Zach felt himself an unreliable proposition, even as uncle. He would remain a houseguest, a detachable presence, courteous, charming, but holding out on them, keeping them safe from the worst effects of loss. That wasn't much to offer a child, that kind of safety from oneself. Furthermore, it surprised him, the strength of his conviction of the danger.

Zach looked about him for his charges, trying to locate them by the glow from the cases: the repulsive scenes of reptile life. Everywhere there were beady eyes and slow movements, sand and dead branches, black puddles under fluorescent light. But among the watchers, no child he knew.

He backtracked and searched again. He walked towards the exit and up the stairs to the daylit world outside, waited, then descended, avoiding the thinning crowds as they pressed past him, children and parents heading home. Soon the reptile house was empty. He walked through it once more till he found an attendant in uniform, beside a small table with a mug of tea and plate of biscuits.

"We're closing. You heard the bell."

"I'm looking for two boys, about seven and ten years old," Zach said.

The attendant stirred the sugar in his cup slowly. He drank his tea. Zach stood and waited.

"There are a lot of boys about seven and ten years old. How did you manage to lose them?"

"They can't be lost, they must be here somewhere."

"Where, exactly?" The man indicated the size of the place with a pale biscuit, "There's nowhere here."

"They wouldn't just leave. Surely there's some place. . . ."

"They're not here. I've just told you that. Unless," he dipped his biscuit in the tea, "one of the pythons got them."

Zach smiled at the grim joke. "Thanks," he said.

"Ask at the gates, I should," the old man called after him. "They're probably wondering where you've got to."

It had been dark and silent in the reptile house, now it was getting dark outside. Almost no one was about. Yet all around him he heard the small noises of penned animals, and of squirrels and birds who walked in and out of the cages, calling to each other, the free beckoning the caught, the confined enticing the free. From the lion house came a long, unmistakably sexual bellowing. In the wild, this was the hour of the hunt, the dusk raids of the carnivores. Perhaps in their cages the antelopes, leaf eaters, paused, alerted by the sound, remembering their dread of what the darkness held. All around him now came scratches and rustlings of creatures inside their incomprehensible captivity, stricken perhaps, as they heard the roars, by the natural panic, yet unable to run, constantly alerted and bored, unable to escape the safety. Projecting anxiety in the life around him, Zach came close to panic himself as he made his way along the paths towards the exit, looking into the shadows for signs of Mick and Willis coming towards him.

He could hold on to nothing, he told himself, take care of no one. Zach hurried onwards, reproaching himself, beginning to call out into the darkness, sending his cries over the rails into the dens of the animals around him, his own sound of creaturely panic, a mother calling to her cubs, or more like, the fallen zebra, attacked by its predator, calling out in terror and warning both.

Get a hold, Zach cautioned himself. This is London. Signposts. In the dark, Zach squinnied at little boards that pointed him towards apes and restrooms. Ahead lay vast plains of elk and giraffe, behind him the tigers. He stood still and calmed himself. Suppose those two are home right now drinking cocoa in front of the TV? Suppose Mick got into a cab an hour ago, or called Michael to come and pick them up? They'd be safe, and Zach would still look a fool. Well, Zach was a fool.

Calm, calm. Zach sat on a bench and tried to listen for sounds of traffic that might direct him to the main gates. The heating pumps, electric generators thumped and buzzed around him, disguising other noises. But above the huge birdcages at the high end of the zoo, Zach saw the skyline of North London, making a halo over the treetops far in the distance.

He walked slowly in this direction, until turning the corner of a large compound, he could make out the lights of the main gates fifty yards away. Approaching, he saw figures in the lodge house, and two shapes of promising height standing against the light.

He slowed down and warned himself not to be angry. "Do you have any idea . . ." he began.

"We were here," Mick said. "Willis needed the loo."

"Why didn't you tell me?"

"We couldn't find you," Willis said, unrepentant. "I had to go."

A large woman in a pink sweater smiled at Zach through the glass partition of the entrance lodge. "Little misadventure?" she said, beaming at them. "They've been so patient, standing about in the dark, not the least worried about you.

Better take them home, I would. Lights go out in twenty minutes."

Zach sat in the cab that took them back, feeling foolish, shameful as Mick rambled on to Willis football gossip, patter that seemed to Zach a generous attempt to pretend that nothing had happened, no fault in him detected. And the performance continued once they were home. He might have counted on Willis's indifference to him to produce just a little snideness, a little joke at his expense that would leave him feeling less utterly outcast by their clear need to protect him. But what had happened remained buried under a conventional account of their day, Helen's consequent gratitude to Zach, Zach's inability to call them on the falsity of their dealings with him.

Only Michael, whose peevishness had to do with Zach's night out, seemed to have an acceptable view of his brother. For the moment, Zach welcomed, felt embraced by, Michael's possessive disapproval.

When the boys were in bed and Helen upstairs with them, Zach watched Michael trying to broach the subject of himself and Anne, felt it looming as Michael attempted to distract himself, carrying business reports in and out of the kitchen, talking to himself, then tossing his brother Xerox copies, clippings, finally handing him a batch of glossy prints. Snatching these away, he angrily reshuffled them before returning them to Zach. "You're a reasonably affluent female under the age of fourteen," Michael said finally. "Which of these is going to get you to accept the horrors of menstruation?"

Zach looked at him.

"This one," Michael said, holding it out with one hand and jabbing at it with a cigarette. "This one says, 'Hey, kid, congratulations, welcome to the wonderful world of carnal knowledge.' OK? See, she's unafraid, this kid, been waiting to get it off since she was five. So it's some kind of diploma. OK," he dropped the photo, picked up another, "here we have for the practical lady, no bits, no bother, no mortifying bulges—right? We zoom in on the nightmare. We could do this more grotesque—back view of the kid in white trousers—only it lacks delicacy. OK, so, or this one that coaxes them into it, you know, try it, if you don't like it, it may go away. This is called Be Prepared, just in case, try it on for size. We use the Mummies in this one, dressing up like Mummy. But it hasn't got the urgency, the bite of doom the others have. Or," Michael fumbled with his clippings, "see, here, this one appeals to pride of possession. They get to focus on the holder. Room of teenie *chatchkas*, horse trophies, rock posters—then, on the table top along with the perfume and punk memorabilia, these trendy mini-pads with their own decorator laminate holders: Pop 'em in your bag, set 'em on the table, symbol of status." Michael reshuffled the photos and dropped them back into Zach's lap. "So choose," he said.

"This one," Zach said wearily, "the welcome."

"What a sentimental slob. You read the statistics, didn't you, anorexic tendencies, fear of the body, you're talking threatening stuff. What would Karen go for?"

Zach thought about this. He didn't even know whether

she had her periods yet or how her body had changed. It happened usually during the summer. She might have come back from her vacation spinning in hormone cycles. Out of the garden, into the wilderness.

"All right," Zach conceded. "Maybe not congratulations, what about some condolence." Zach tried to appease Michael by mimicking the manner: "It had to happen sometime, we can help you face it."

"That's a little down-mouthed," Michael said, startled, "but not so bad. Maybe we could work it, you know, more sardonically. The wry-smiling mother, glamorous type, letting the kid into those nasty-beautiful mysteries. Yeah, that's good, Zach, she's got a kind of joke with the daughter: 'Bad luck, honey,' then she shoves the pack at her." Michael took the materials from Zach and dropped them onto a chair next to the sideboard, came back and sat down.

"So did you like my friend?"

"Who?"

"You know who."

Michael turned his head and looked around the kitchen as though searching for something, then he twisted in his chair. "You must forgive my un-Englishness. I only say one thing. As a native of London and knowing your stay is shortish, I wouldn't want you to waste your time. For example, I do not suggest you visit the Tower of London while you're here, nor Madame Tussaud's. And I do not suggest you get too involved with Miss or rather Mrs. Newhouse—I believe she still retains the name of her most recent life companion."

87

"She's not Zsa Zsa Gabor, Michael, she's only been married twice."

"Probably only twice, yeah. Anyway," Michael said, getting up and beginning to pace, "when are you seeing her again, if I'm not prying?"

"Not prying, bludgeoning. Tuesday. Is that all right with you?"

"It's your funeral."

"I'm a big boy now, Michael."

"Yeah. Big boy in a shaky state, whose domestic life has recently moved from cyclone stage to dust bowl. You come here asking for peace and brotherly stabilization and at the first offer of guidance you go precisely against the advice. My simple suggestion is that you may not yet be out of the woods enough to take on another Queen of Darkness. Why *do* you go for them?"

"You realize you're making her irresistible?"

"Well, there's my point right there."

"For godsake, Michael, how wobbly do you think I am?"

"How wobbly do *you* think you are is more the point. And her, too."

Helen came downstairs. They were silent.

"The air is very thick in here," Helen said.

"No. Everybody's up, right, Zach?"

Michael moved towards his wife. Soon they were talking about the boys and the week. Zach sat still and watched them.

One night that week Zach waited for Anne at a restaurant near to where, as she told him, she had to "look in" on a drinks party. She would have brought him if she could, she said, but it was "impossible." By ten she had still not arrived, and Zach sat conspicuously alone and unserved, while around him elegant groups ordered dishes with great seriousness, and consumed them with great laughter. The place Anne had chosen was not a place for private encounters, Zach noted. Nor for outsiders. Every individual belonged to his party and all the parties to this restaurant. There were no accidents or strays. The diners took their good fortune as their due, and the waiters, responsive to the sense of decorum, were comfortable, respectful, unnaturally cheerful. Zach, not only American, but unaccompanied, they left alone, invisible, and unincorporated. He broke his bread and observed the life around him, unworried. When Anne arrived, he would be admitted to the festivities. By now, he understood enough of how it worked. No slobbering democratic familiarity New York style, from unemployed actors to expense-account outsiders, here there was a society, as Michael said, for everything.

Anne arrived eventually, flushed and in high mood. Zach watched how her familiarity with the place dictated her entrance. The headwaiter confirmed Zach's sense of it. That he had been waiting for Anne, Zach could see, now accorded him high and certain status. Zach stood as Anne had her coat removed by one attentive waiter and strode towards him on high spiked heels, dressed in black and silver silks, like some fabulous machine of war.

"Zach, I'm so sorry to keep you. I just couldn't get away." She said this as she kissed him, one cheek among the recent multitude, but with an exuberance that dismissed the subject of her lateness, buried it under a gust of scent and hair and skin, and more than a trace of cocktails.

Other diners turned to look, marked, accepted them, and returned gratified to their meals.

"You do look wonderful," Zach told her.

"Thank you." Anne sat down, and restlessly looked about her in the large room. He could see she was still at the drinks party, herself a gay and passive screen onto which other people would project in short succession, in pieces. Zach waited for her to settle, disturbed by the idea of his own disappointing nonplurality, unhappy to be the gloomier part of her evening.

"Would you like a drink?" he asked.

"I've had lots to drink, what about you?" She smiled at him and continued to survey the room.

"Certainly." Zach signaled.

The waiters descended on them now, brought them wine and took their orders. Anne began to relax into her evening, seemed to accept no one else was going to arrive, that she was alone with Zach.

Zach, too, began to relax, and find a continuation of Anne—such as he knew her—inside the phenomenon that sat across from him.

"You had fun tonight?" She was sinking a little, he thought he should remind her of her recent triumphs.

"I had fun," Anne admitted and smiled, possessor of power in a world where only some people got to have fun. "And I'm sorry I couldn't take you, and made you wait, though maybe if you'd come I wouldn't have had so much fun."

"Too honestly said," Zach laughed.

"Well I like to go on my own, especially when I'm in the doubly good position of being able to escape somewhere after. No one can stick to me," Anne said happily. "And I see all those wives and husbands eyeing their spouses across the room, knowing that no matter how good a time they're having, their manner of leaving is fixed, that the present freedom is an illusion. So they envy me, which I rather like, though sometimes they pretend they're worried about me. I enjoy the envy, notwithstanding my freedom is as much a charade as theirs."

"Meaning: because you were fated to end the evening with me?"

"Not at all. Because everyone is stuck. Some just get to blame it on their partners."

The food arrived. Anne finished her wine and Zach filled

her glass. He guessed that this was as far as she would go with this revelation.

"Do you flirt with the husbands?" Zach asked.

"They flirt with me," Anne said defensively.

"That goes without saying."

She softened a little.

"I can't finish." A gesture from Karen, she pushed the plate towards him. She'd eaten almost nothing, too speedy for her first course, which Zach, ravenous by the time it arrived, had finished for her.

"You should eat something."

"You mean I shouldn't be drinking on an empty stomach," Anne laughed. The laughter warned him she didn't want him so close. It was her style, he saw, to offer him roles to play with her, then take them away. Now he tried to wrest control by ignoring her game. Confused, she started again, more neutrally, resuming their distance.

"What did you do today?"

"I went to the British Museum to look at musical manuscripts. They don't make much effort to display things, do they?"

"I think they feel it's up to the public to make the effort."

"Well, consequently perhaps, there wasn't much public there, a few tramps."

"Scholars, probably."

"And then I wandered around Bloomsbury, past the immortal dwellings, walked back to Hampstead."

"A long walk."

"Nice. I nearly got run over a couple of times. Then I

watched television with Willis and Mick, then I did some shopping for Helen."

"This does not seem like a full day for a grown man."

"That's what Willis said. When I went out to get cigarettes, though, a nice thing happened. You want to hear?"

"All right." Anne was docile again. She finished her drink and sat back to listen.

"You know how they make you wait in every shop here, well they do. So I was standing with my magazine trying to get this girl just to reach behind her and hand me a pack of Marlboros so I could pay and go, but she was having a long phone call and I couldn't get her attention. I became very British and patient, read my magazine about twelve inches in front of her nose. Finally she puts the phone down. I lower my magazine, and she says 'moment.' I think, Oh Christ, what now. But she says it again, and this time I notice how elated she is. 'Moment.' "

" 'Moment?' " Anne asks him.

"Yes, then she focuses and turns to me, 'man of the moment,' she says and does a little dance and pats the phone. 'Oh,' I say, and she looks at me again. Then she says: 'It's so *easy* to be happy.' "

"And what did you say to that?"

"What can you say to that, I thought it was wonderful."

"Must have been very young this girl," Anne said.

"Or very smart," Zach said.

"You think so?" Anne said.

Zach on Helen's flowered sheets woke inside the blackout of London nighttime, damp, dream-asphixiated, his lungs heavy, his head jagged, rocks over which a surf pounded. The pounding came from his heart and his dreams, where his past danced whorishly, promising that all would be well, that nothing had changed. He dreamed his mother's face, and his own, and a briary hillside that led down to the sea. Maine, an expedition for blackberries. Zach was eight. A dark, thick wickered basket stroked his mother's long, pale-cotton-covered thigh where they walked, the blackberries heavy inside, darker, dull under the late afternoon sun. All around them the small farms and scraggy hillsides as summer was ending, and the sea that beat against the rocks below. Coexistence: mother, child, sea, walking home, up the hillside. Zach wary, looked for snakes: his mother would not protect him. Little man, Zach. Little nervous man.

Those you've loved you always love. There is no peace from that. Nighttime reminders, debt-collecting, Zach re-

94

harnessed. Not free, he belonged. Once, sheltering in the soft of his mother's breast and belly, as her spine curved a shell around him, a smell of tides and breathing. Seaflesh, a color, living, palpitating, unconscious. Closer to the sea inside Maggie, ebb, flow, beaching home. Desire to be lost thus in conchflesh and chalkspine. The mermaids would drown him. Zach pulled himself from his bed, breathed deeply his own stale air, lit a cigarette. Three A.M. No time to be awake in London.

Bad habit was all there was to hold on to. He poured the whiskey he kept by his bed, smoked his cigarette, looked at nothing outside his window but his own poor reflection. Now again the images sailed in front of him like cheap theater props: a wafting mirage of Maggie, the pang that called him with his daughter's voice, almost entirely pain now, equation of Karen and self-reproach until he resisted thinking of her. If he could think of her with joy simply, simply as he sometimes dreamed her, or of Maggie. Of whom now did he think in such a way that the thinking was only pleasure, the way the old are meant to think, creaking on their porches, the sunny days passing under wizened brows, lips moving to ancient tunes? Only Anne, sex object, strumpeting morality-free for an instant. That was what attraction was, the lie of pleasure only, an una-dulterated thought, tinselly, unlike all other, history-laden, thoughts. Time would take care of it. Already Zach was spoiling, scrutinizing, knew Anne was not a kümmel to be tasted. Moral baggage and wariness. Zach scouting for snakes in paradise.

Why this one now? This infinitely unsuitable one. Anne's

theory, love in a moving vehicle? Was he a field made to lie fallow according to predetermined plan, springing again in dumb response to someone else's season? Why not in New York? Why had he never got beyond desire, loving his own desires, stopping there, discarding, self-sickened, spent? He had wanted something from those women. He had come to them burdened with demands. He had wanted each other one to be a stop for him, silence. And yet the change and music of change had kept him going, pursuing, fleeing: a poor wooden animal on a carousel. He didn't know why this was different. Because he wanted nothing? Or could expect so little? Because he did not choose her; not knowing her, did not love her for herself, but as a sign almost, form of all the others he had ever loved. But, still, why her? Because the pain was a crack that let the truth through? Glimpse of the eternal under the ragged defense. Love, then, a possibility with every woman? Yes, except that Anne now had signaled him. Her pain, or the despair (his own) that had led him to listen.

Round and round his thoughts took him, but his feelings led him straight. Simplemindedly he followed, like Hansel with Gretel in the forest.

Anne and Maggie, a double act. Cabaret girls: Loss and Desire. Between them he was stretched taut like the string of a harp, hearing new melodies, making them. What was over and what had not begun, his arms widened to span these points, infinite, and only self-wide. Zach was the measure: the present, his edges touching theirs; his own past, Maggie's; his own future, Anne's. There was no reason to suppose that Anne and he had a future, no reason except that he felt the stretch, the blood rushing back to the muscle, life to the bone. I am alive. Pain and desire tell me so.

There were messages all over. There were signs and sensations. Nothing made sense but to surrender expectation of sense, shut up and listen. It was a strange life. It seemed rich to him, as though turning corners, hearing snatches of song, smelling summer earth in the middle of winter. People that he loved came and went all day long, as haphazard as colors, breezes of the dead, the living absent faces, those loved, those barely registered. New York and London melded, overlapped, separated, fused.

There's no there there, they say about America. But in London, New York seeped back to him, its images beckoning beyond this city's corners. Sometimes he almost forgot where he was, set off for a place three thousand miles away. Or daydreaming in London, a layer would lift and New York show herself, a glimpse of cityflesh, no more than a bunionworth, hipflash, and then be gone.

Here, he thought about there. With her, them, he thought of Maggie and Karen. Not even thought about, felt them present in these new presences, as though there were no distinction between persons, between places, as though the present were only a face of the past. At times Anne would become for him all women, all stages of the woman he'd most loved: Maggie in the beginning, Maggie as young mother of Karen, Karen herself. He could see in her only a different form of something that was constant, always there, always would be there. When Maggie was an old woman, this thing would be seen in Karen. Anne's children would have it. Having her, he could hold them all. Loving her was the key to these loves regained. Novelty had led him to the place where nothing changes—the Don Juan's boast: loving a thousand, I am the soul of fidelity. High, sleepless, idle in London, he felt in possession once more of all he'd ever lost: Those you've loved you always love.

One thing about being alive, if you stayed that patiently, there would be surprises. Maggie, for example, had decided to resume contact. At first the letters came in short and ironical, practical, guarded. A small note enclosing a long letter from Karen, a message from Zach's mother relayed without comment, a dentist's reminder forwarded and forwarded again. Then, increasingly, tender phrases hemmed these notes: Are you really all right? Don't stay away forever. We think of you and miss you—that *we* royal certainly, and royally armed: Karen and Maggie, the left-at-homes. Their missives grew larger, harder to slide in drawers and fuse with the chaos of the present. Karen's sketches, no longer touchingly wobbly, but accomplished, eager to please, no longer happy with the approximation of things, but personality-censored, in hot pursuit of a technically proficient, commonly agreed-upon mimesis. Maggie sent photos of them both, and then as though after some decision, began to write him real letters, reaching out to him less and less archly, intimate even, as he strayed further, began to make his own stumbling peace with their separation, as though Zach in absentia had become someone to trust. Following the letters came snippets of diary, unsigned, inexplicable, and unexplained. Perhaps out of some instinct to keep him she'd switched tactics, or simply abandoned tactics, offered him friendship, a share of her unflinching look. He stuck her Xerox pages in a suitcase and went off to stay with Anne. One day he began to read some of it and recognized not Maggie but an unknown self:

"I am afraid," Maggie wrote. "We should start there. Everything begins with that void. Like fear of falling when you let go of the handrail. But falling itself, as one remembers, is OK. Just the fear, not OK. In the beginning, darkness. Or in the beginning these words. These words enter the darkness and take its place. All will be well.

"I am afraid. I have been afraid these last three years. Two years of running so fast and free I convinced myself. But slowed down, self-stopped, I began to crumble. Like those sci-fi heroes in the last shot, melting, flying apart. I had my own physics, just for me, no gravity, a long space between cause and effect, radio waves that spun around and hit me on the ear. It was when I was so firm on terra firma (I was, you could read it in the industry paper) that I began to come loose. There is no fear like that, like putting your foot through space and waiting light years for it to come down. That funny business didn't go away. I ran, back to where the childhood terrors are, then back again to New York, ran to jobs and home again, back to the papers that explained where you were and how you fitted in, back to my place, manless, fraudulent, but given me as my own.

"Listen, if I'd had the choice, wouldn't I have lingered? I say I was an exhausted traveler, willing to check into this hotel or that hotel, happy, I say, to pay and stop, take my sauna, hang out at the bar, watch a sunset, sleep till noon.

"It's not as though I chose to be fussy. Just that there was no rest ever, in the end, in those places, and I was forced to go on. I never wanted to be this pilgrim, no matter what I told Zach, never wanted to get further and further into the wild places. I didn't choose. It just happened that I could not stop anymore, couldn't get the rest. I'd wave my checkbook everywhere: I'm willing, show me the room. I tested the beds, unpacked for a long stay. But something changes and you're not allowed to stop. Something keeps you moving. God knows, not my idea of a holiday.

"Fidgeting pilgrim. This man and that man, and this city and that job, all hotels where you couldn't ever stop, though the rest was promised. So now we merely revise our idea of travel.

"I long for oblivion. The stupidest line I ever read was in Anaïs Nin's memoirs: 'Consciousness is the great blessing.' Yes, but what if you can't take it in more than teaspoon doses? One second a day. Except that avoiding it becomes more exhausting in the end than surrender, who would not choose to swallow their drugs?

"I'm scared. If nothing more than just sitting here is what there is. I want my illusions: progress, comfort, eternal love. I'll freeze to death. Other people must be here for a reason, I mean use. I don't like this outer space. I sit and watch David and exchange observations. This is not love, this is space-companions. I am beyond rape fantasies, or am I? (Ladylike rape fantasies, *je vous assure*.) This mutual respect, so philosophically right, so extraordinarily generous, leaves the id out of it, or not the id, the part that wants shelter, safety, and orgasms.

"But orgasms come detached from this, isn't that the point? Why all the artists go for floozies, sexual exercise for the id, solitude for the refined being at the top, refined being taken off to dream in the studio, rub up against a word processor, saving it all for something that counts. Too bleak, too bleak, this future. I want to turn back. Yet I don't want no deaf dumb love, no banker, no job hound, no accumulator of property. I want my angel to be a sexual angel. I want a new bestiary.

"It's good for the art, they tell you, the not having forces you to invent. Why all those writers give you frostbite: feeling for the pages only. David the Considerate. Well, no gain without pain as they say in the gyms. The blinded songbirds and all that. But for what sitcom spot am I being prepared by such hard times? Where do I get to use what I know, if not in love? The door of the hotel room slams: I see the towels laid out and the welcome planter's punch. I know I shall have departed in the morning. My, you do put up a fight, dearie. It's a gift, you know."

He found himself embarrassed by what she seemed to ask of him. Perhaps only his ear, more or less randomly chosen, sea-separated, Atlantic-safe. Did she send copies to David, this writer? artist? the space-giver? Or only to him, invited to stick his finger in the wound. He found his old response: the puffing chest, refusal of guilt, refusal of pain. All this is behind me now. He pictured Anne to himself, lit a cigarette or made a call. Still Maggie crept through. He worried about Karen. *None of this is my fault.*

He crept down to Helen. In her silence she seemed an ally. That privacy of hers became his shrine; he worshiped at the lake of her contentment. Tell me, he wished to ask, how this is done, this painless life of yours, this life of so little? He watched her closely: she shopped, she cooked, she spoke to her children and friends. In the afternoons she lay on her bed reading. In the evenings Michael took over. The life hardly seemed sufficient explanation.

And yet she existed somewhere beyond even curiosity as to what lay out there, buffeting, terrorizing Maggie. Or had Helen been and returned? Her containment spoke of knowledge, choices, renunciation as deprivation transformed. The odd thing was the way there was no whine to her, no whiff of sour grapes. But the mystery was how it was done.

Once in Vatican City, Maggie and he had gone to a pharmacy. While Zach looked through the sunglasses and postcards of John XXIII, she bent towards the young chemist, explained the gynecological problem in latinate and broken English, sotto voce, to avoid the ears of the tweeded English, the nuns from New Jersey, the red-nosed priests from County Clare. Understanding, the chemist translated for her: *Lei ha dolore quando va con un uomo.* Yes, that was it. Maggie had pain when she went with a man.

Zach went with Anne to a performance of *The Winter's Tale.* He sat in his seat imagining that Maggie was thawing out for him like Hermione, that the recent years of stoniness had been punishment undertaken for his own good. Reconciliation (with the lost daughter, too) might follow. But he stalled at the notion, allowed himself the memory of old battles. Would it even be comfortable living again with Karen, clearly moving at good pace towards the conventional, grown-up–appeasing life of earliest adolescence, when panicky deals are made, intended to forestall the storms of sensation, the thumping demands of unique selfhood, when cowering in social saneness you demand a breather, attempt to con the primal gods? Innocent love, sporting now on stage in buskin and flowerlets—was there ever such a time? Wasn't it always both insufficient and overwhelming? Didn't one always do it wrong—lacking courage, lacking faith? Or had the idea always been really so simple as simply to keep going?

He glanced at Anne, chin tilted into the stage light, calm under the stately makeup, soothed by the comedy. He took her hand where the darkness hid it. The king was on again, lost in extravagant gloom.

Zach had not often seen Maggie on stage. She did her regional work without him, without much audience, encouragement, zest. But once he'd watched her in *A Month in the Country*. She had moved him to tears. Or Turgenev. He remembered his envy of the writer, the unmenaced quality of his knowledge of women. His was a freedom Zach thought he'd never had.

The audience was laughing and clapping now, roused by the dancing cockney Autolycus. A vaudeville encore loosened the grip of the early scenes, wherein Zach had witnessed, in the poisonous actions of the king, his own senseless obsessive undertakings, futilely aimed at the relief of love.

They stood and filed out among the slow-weaving, self-conscious audience. They made for the bar, suddenly crowded by the panicky polite insinuating themselves in the direction of the bottles. Zach jutted a shoulder forward and waited his turn. Around him, white-cuffed hands stretched from jackets to press notes on the barman. Again he watched the elaborate social instruction, watched his own patience rewarded, his right to speak granted wordlessly by the faintest official nod in his direction.

He clutched their drinks and a fistful of ice cubes and turned tightly from the crowd. He apologized his way outwards, looking for Anne among the waiting women at the far end of the room; plump shoulders in dark sleeves gestured around him, greetings burst on the air as the room was crossed, recognitions claimed.

"Zach," Anne's voice raised itself like a sunflower above the hedges of talkers. She was in the company of a tall man, expensively dressed, darkly tanned, in his early fifties. "This is my ex-husband Sam Newhouse," she said. "And this is Zach Quine, Michael's brother."

Sam removed his hand from her back and offered it. "A great pleasure," he said.

Zach kept his distance and bowed. With his right fist he indicated the thawing ice cubes and an inability to shake hands.

"Have this," Sam held out a soft, ironed handkerchief, shaking it out so Zach would take it.

"Sam always has hundreds," Anne said.

"So useful in England. Not a nation given much to paper napkins, nor free matches or carrier bags for that matter, and modern life can be so messy."

Zach refolded the cotton square with one hand against his chest and downed his drink with the other.

"Where's your drink?" Anne asked.

"Not worth the trip to the bar," Sam said. "Besides, I don't much these days." They looked at each other, challenging.

"Sam's just back from Johannesburg, hence the brilliant tan."

Sam smiled. "And you," he said, "here for a while?"

"A little break from New York," Zach said, "visiting Michael." He looked at Anne, she was wishing him well.

"We were saying how good Paulina is, or is said to be. Her moment, of course, is later. Your wife is an actress, I believe Michael mentioned, Shakespearean?"

"Not often," Zach said. He tried to take a position with them, rescue his wife, surprise someone. Giving up, he accepted his role as laconic Yankee and looked about him like a tourist. In the far corner, a crone in lace collar and black nylon uniform took charge of a counter of chocolates and sickly looking orange drinks that sat warming on a buffet in square plastic containers. By her side a maroon-jacketed official monitored a row of bottles under a dusty glass-framed list of prices. The floors sloped under worn red carpet, walls listed under yellowing posters of ancient productions. All this might have come unaltered from Sickert's day, nothing like the chauvinism of the Present in New York, those anxiety-ridden declarations—in gleaming surfaces, polished counters, spot-lit posters—that this place, this production, this very moment is the latest thing.

It was getting harder not to slide into Englishness. It crept humidly around him, seeped into him. All this was seeming familiar. Not so the foreground figures: this bronze-haired woman, propelled by nerves, never quiet but perpetually bright, evading capture, and her companion, solidly still, sun-browned, affable, eloquent of manners and substance, now cunning, now enticed. Her laughter was an act of questioning, addressing them both. With Zach, it faltered as though she did not know him—but this was only a feint for Sam, a sexual provocation in such a mime of modesty: backing down even in this so modest a demand that Zach respond to her happiness. And then her husband's laughter, sidesteppingly gracious, like a deposition of favors, coins spilled from a limousine window to urchins on the street. Comforting to be around him, ownership conceded not resented. And here they all were together, she in her laughter asking, Sam withholding and bestowing, and he, Zach, watching and smiling, and locked into affability.

"I must be getting back to my little group," Sam said, turning to him, "I just came over to tell Anne how beautiful she looks. Perhaps we shall meet at Michael's." He held out his hand. "Do say hello. Enjoy the play," he signaled them as he moved off slowly, stately as from the helm of a yacht. They waved back, already smaller figures on the dock.

"My husband," Anne said when they were alone.

"I got that. A handsome man."

"Sam? Wonderful eyes, hasn't he?"

"You seem very friendly."

"Yes? And why not?" You don't own me, she said. I doubt if you could even understand.

The crowd swirled around them, pressed them forward. Ahead, Sam and his party of five slid silken backs into orchestra seats. The theater lights caught the gleam of silver cloth and silver hair as they dimmed into darkness.

Later, at dinner, in acts of reconciliation, she fed him pieces of Sam.

"Sam is in stones," she said, "diamonds. I met him through

some South African friends. He was charming, not English, which I thought then was what was needed. It was when I was with him I learned to make jewelry. He left his stones around the house. He's successful, you know."

"You mean rich."

"Rich then, like a cake." She turned about her in the restaurant, registering irritation.

Zach leaned forward. "Tell me about him."

"I was trying to."

"Not his income."

"I thought I was speaking to an American. Don't you always ask what people do?"

"Not this American."

"Oh yes, unemployed. How tactless."

He waited for her.

She said, "Tell me about your wife."

"She writes to me."

"Really."

"Only recently."

"And what is she like?"

Zach looked at her, thinking how to answer.

"You see? Why should I tell? It's an ordinary question. But you like everyone else will judge me accordingly. Sam is wonderful," she said defiantly, "I didn't marry him for his money."

Zach waited.

"He loved me and we lived together, fairly happily. No, we were never happy. He wanted to save me and I wouldn't let him. I never forgave him for leaving his wife, though once he'd done it that was really the reason we married. Later I came to feel he'd blackmailed me that way, tried to make me take his love seriously."

"And why didn't you 'take his love seriously'?"

"Because he was so used to getting his way. Because of the money. I wouldn't take it and it hurt him. He felt I left him alone with his crimes. Unwifely."

"What crimes?"

"Just the normal crimes of the business world, nothing illegal."

"You are romantic about money."

"I was romantic about marriage."

"I see."

"You don't see. You don't know me."

"You keep saying that. You keep your privacy and reproach me for it."

"But you are the same," she said. "Exactly the same, a dog with two masters. Two whistles: love and freedom. A dog touches with his nose before he runs away, only a game, and for you, too, a game, wanting to leave and wanting to stay. Why *do* you stay?"

"To find out what people want," Zach said simply. "I ask people I'm attracted to what it is they want. They describe something so small as to be absurd."

"And yet?" Anne said.

"And yet," Zach continued, "more and more it seems to be the strength of the appetite that counts, the quality of the greed. For the good things."

"Yes?" Anne said. "Yes, and what are they? Begin again,

Zach. A leap of faith. Something must hold you here. Somewhere you must connect. You are a fish struggling, flopping, gasping for air. Always flopping, I hear it."

"Forgive me," she said later. "I have no right to lecture you. I run, too. I run from you and I ran from Sam and I'm only ever treading water."

He felt empowered by these loops of hers, rapid descents into stillness. He watched her now, willing her to let them continue, make something of the moment of exhaustion that held them at a place where movement seemed possible. Her cat curled at her feet, twisting and stretching its neck to soothe a paw, eloquent of endless time and safety. In a moment a word could change them. They waited while it passed, conscious and a little ashamed that they did so.

When he was with her, he held to what he thought was his honesty, what was familiar to him as doubt. Her normal words were no more than singing, jostling, covering them with a way to be silent. To address him she used something other than words. Hearing her speech take back what her expressions confessed, he spoke against her words, comically deaf to them. She was confused when he did this, she'd been successful with language too long.

Next to his loneliness in New York, this often seemed a crueler form of solitude. Zach thought that only when their words meant the same as what they said with their bodies and eyes would they be whole and free to move.

He thought it was smart to make some sign of his intention to take London (and likewise Anne) seriously. He thought it was wise not to outstay his welcome at Michael and Helen's. He thought it would be fun to live like a free man in London, in a large empty room into which he might bring a piano. He went to the agencies, where they looked him over skeptically. It was his age and solitude that bothered them, that and his so-called self-employment. They offered him must-smelling basement flats that looked out on dustbins through barred windows. They offered him cluttered flats in Kensington, belonging to elderly single women temporarily away. His Americanness soothed them, as at the same time it confused them. He was not interested, he said, in being "a stone's throw" from Harrod's. He did not perk up at the prospect of a garden. What he wanted, he said, was one large empty room with high ceilings, into which he might fit a piano. "It's a short let," they said, "that will mean furnished." "There are neighbors," they said, "we don't know about a piano."

Helen tried to help. She suggested bedrooms in the homes of friends, but seemed relieved when he declined these offers. It was as though her responsibility stretched so far might involve them in things precarious. In any case, there was small chance of a piano.

The ex-wife of a friend in New York was moving back. Her flat would be almost empty by the time she left. "It's not much," she told him, "one large room and a bath, but it's cheap, and the neighbors are never there." He saw the flat one morning while she was packing. It was just what he wanted.

Now he sat waiting for Rachel and the keys at a coffee bar near the British Museum. Rachel had been working there for the past four years on a doctorate, the money for which had been her divorce settlement from Jack. Jack had an idea that Rachel was really there to find an English husband. "Nobody in their right mind gets a Ph.D. at forty-five," he said. "Nobody in their right mind gives two farts about the literary output of Frieda Lawrence. Frieda's contribution to literature has already been recognized. It was to drive D.H. into his books. I have myself spoken on this theme ad infinitum. In fact you might say it is the basis of a larger theory of aesthetics: life in the form of unsavory marriages, heartless landlords, club feet, weak chests, and general all-around unfitness and misery as the grit that makes the pearl. Art is an act of compensation. It comes of deprivation and longing. Frieda and England, of course, provided the first, D.H. through travel and memory cultivated the second. The idea of Frieda's red pencil and helpful suggestions is not only laughable but in Rachel a form of transferred megalomania. I'm not surprised it's taking forever for her to work up her little thesis. Let's hope she comes back with an earl."

Now under a yellowing photo-mural of Portofino, inside the fog of an espresso machine, Zach sat with his cup, powder blue as a bathroom tile, watching the brown, separating liquid lap over the sides when the underground rumbled.

Rachel was late. "McCafferty's widow," Jack McCafferty called her, describing her thus even before the divorce and its attendant recriminations. Once Rachel had moved to London, the grizzled playwright had softened somewhat towards his former muse and one night late on Hudson Street had extracted Zach's promise to look her up. "You always lusted after her," Jack said somewhat tragically. In deference to the older man's feelings Zach had simulated a lecherous grin and nodded his head, as though to acknowledge a stunning perspicacity in his old friend. The New York bar check with Rachel's number scrawled on it he had accepted in wordless acknowledgment of the sexual transfer. It lay before him now on the chipped Formica, creased and pink as an infant's palm.

"Who are these awful people?" McCafferty had demanded the night he gave him her number. He used his booming voice, a provocation straight from the heroic days of the Cedar Bar. He swung his shaggy head violently, snorting like a snared bison, his brown eyes glistening. "Yerps and yuppies," he would say, referring (in the terminology of Ezra Pound) to the invading Euro-trash on the one hand

and (in the terminology of yuppies themselves) to the lo-
botomized local consuming young on the other. The former, fearful of communism at home, had taken over the
city, installed security systems to keep out the native free-
lance capitalists, and paid the rents that, escalating to horrendous sums in the last ten years, had driven the virtuous
aborigines into the cracks and corners of the town, where
like McCafferty they clung, spitting venom, to rent-
controlled gold-dust, not very safe apartments. The native
invaders, overgroomed and bland as television, insultingly
young and insultingly affluent, were likewise entrenched in
the city, driving up its rents and out its poets, and making,
together with the foreigners, New York a rich man's town;
and, hence to Jack, issuing in the death of the place as a
place where art is made.

"You can trace," he said, "the decline of the American
soul in that of its national game. From baseball: tragic,
Greek, heroic to Monopoly: Manifest Destiny and Babbit-
try."

"And now?" Zach said.

"Didn't you listen to those kids you taught? The game's
called Trivial Pursuit."

That night, as the aliens sat around them in seersucker
and Giorgio Armani, torturing him with their discussions
of movies and restaurants, he had taunted them: "The business of America is business," he'd say. Or again and again,
more helplessly, "Who *are* these people?"

They ignored him. He was now wallpaper, part of the
historical color they came to the bar for. Some of them

might have recognized the playwright, but deference was alien to them. Jack felt, and made Zach feel, like a member of a dying breed: old and foolish bohemia, not like this present bunch, the arts and media mob with their processed thoughts on processed culture.

"Carvel," Jack would shout at them, "Carvel heads."

No sign of Rachel. She was now half-an-hour late. That was her style, as he remembered, breeze in, breeze out, free as a breeze. She wouldn't own a watch. Jack was wrong, Zach had never lusted after her. That independence of hers was no accident.

The door of the café opened and two small boys entered in front of a middle-aged man dragging a pram. Behind him two older boys scuffled and argued and came to a stop inside the room. They were all a little dirty, the baby wild-eyed, his skin chapped, the adult unshaven and frayed at the cuffs.

Over the espresso machine the owner hailed them as they slid noisily into a booth. A tall and beautiful daughter, with Botticelli locks, gave them menus and addressed them in broad cockney. Under the table his sons kicked each other's feet while the exhausted papa bounced the pram and peered at its occupant.

"So how is Mrs.?" the Italian shouted over the steam.

"A daughter finally." They laughed, the Italian daughter, too.

"Spaghetti and chips?" the father said. "How many?" He pointed a dirty menu at his party, counted them off and included the baby. Orange drinks the color of defoliant, a plate of stacked white bread slices, and soft pats of butter arrived with the dinners. Lovingly and wearily, the father spread the pasta onto the Wonder Bread, folded it carefully, and placed the sandwich between the dirty hands of his youngest son.

Watching the scene, wondering about paternal helplessness, Zach failed to notice Rachel standing before him, a battered briefcase in her hand.

When he first saw her a week ago he would not have recognized her. She seemed taller and older—by about ten years. Still, you'd have to say the years had been good to her, or that since she'd left Jack she'd made up for lost time. She had a kind of focus now, fatigue with cunning. He'd remembered her as more of a background figure, but perhaps that was Jack's theatrical upstaging.

"How's Maggie?" she'd asked first thing. Zach remembered why he'd never "lusted" after her. Too direct, the kind that can read your thoughts and make you guilty before they've registered home.

Harder, was that the difference? Rosier. The hair color was reddish now, and spiked, too, like a picket fence, the look not meant to keep you out but promise you a brawl once you were in. Alleycat Rachel. That was it. The breakup with Jack had unzipped the anger she used to hold inside her like a growl. It surrounded her now like a halo. Joan of Arc. A Woman Alone.

"And you're going home," Zach said when she gave him the keys.

"Yes, finally, God knows why. I shall miss it here and probably regret the move as soon as I make it. I've been back a couple of times, but I always returned to London, never felt tough enough to take it all on. And who can afford it anymore? Even if I get a teaching job, I'll probably have to live in New Jersey. Or share a place. I mean, at my age. I should never have married a writer. Writer's alimony—that and a dollar will get you a ride on the subway."

"Jack seems to think you're living a tourist's fantasy here," Zach mentioned.

"Jack! My London's less of a fantasy than his ghost town of Brendan Behan, Eugene O'Neill, Pollock, and God knows who all dead else."

"So why go?"

"Masochism, no doubt. Maybe once you're used to New York anything civilized seems fake. I'll tell you what it is, Zach, if you want to know. I miss the heroes, I miss the soldiers on the New York battlefield. Here no one has to be brave; it's all so comfortable, the military virtues aren't cultivated. Besides, I think New Yorkers know something that Londoners don't, not just about survival, other things, important. More important than the things they don't know about furniture and wine. Hard to name. Unease. A grown-up sort. Maybe it's only because there aren't enough Jews. No I mean it. It's so solid, London, small and settled, and there's no present. Everything is experienced through the filter of the past. There seems to be a shortage of grown-ups altogether, charming youths and then smug middle-age, and nothing in between. Look at people in the street, the sexiness belongs to the very young, but Paris, New York, people in their thirties and forties, fifties even, are still alive and awake. Remember when they used to make films about grown-ups? They mostly came from France, but that's New York life, too, that staying alive and staying anxious."

"That's exactly what I've had enough of."

"So hang around. London's a great convalescence center for New Yorkers, but in the end you'll head back bleating for what looks like reality. We think we're free in this matter, but we've already been programmed, caught up in the motor that runs the place: doubt and appetite on roller skates, desire in pursuit of illusion. But still," Rachel said, looking out of the window and dramatically indicating the gray beyond, "there are some things there, were, so beautiful that nothing here . . . I never saw anything quite so exciting as the day I wheeled my cart down a supermarket aisle and came across six young firemen standing around the meat counter buying for a barbecue—all of them six foot four in black rubber boots, blue jeans and T-shirts, picking out T-bones and counting on their fingers and letting me by in this shy baby-boy manner. You never saw anything so powerful and young as those blue firemen. I stayed in the store and followed them most of the morning." Rachel sighed. "I find myself here missing even the barrios and the butchers selling cabrito, goat and *salsa* on days when the temperature reaches one hundred and murder's on the agenda. You can get to miss anything when things are quiet enough. The barrio, imagine, Broadway and One Hundred Sixth, and here I sit in Bloomsbury longing for it and those firemen."

"I'm trying to believe you," Zach said.

"Life is rough in New York and it's less rough here. That's

the simple difference, isn't it? I used to think that if you're going to do your own work anyway and live without someone to protect you—though it's not hard to say who protected whom in the ménage of Jack McCafferty—then you might as well take it where it's gentlest, make your own challenges. That makes sense, doesn't it? But then I had to wonder about the long-term effects—and I would ask myself—of all this ease and predictability, of life without those firemen."

"Quite a sacrifice for a glimpse of blue-collar beauty."

"Well, we'll see. Wish me luck, at least. It's not been the easiest decision. Apart from anything else, it's economic suicide going back. That should have made it simple. But it didn't. It's that notion of the edge, isn't it? It makes everything else seem second-rate."

"And if it's just a notion, together with a handful of images?"

"But I think I need to know. Maybe I'm wrong, and maybe you'll find here what I didn't."

He was determined to. He moved into Rachel's room and set up his books on a card table. He hung his few clothes in the cupboard, set his shaving kit in the bathroom, stocked the knee-high fridge and found a place that rented pianos. He put his phone on the table next to his books and sat there looking out over the garden square, placing himself where he would be ready to receive a way to go forward. He tried to suppress the feeling he'd made this kind of move once before.

His daughter was having anxiety attacks. That is what Maggie wrote to him. They had started in the last few weeks and were serious enough to warrant consultation with a psychiatrist.

"We thought at first it was some kind of hay fever or asthma the way she can't catch her breath and gasps for air like a fish out of water. It happens in the middle of nothing in particular, when she's sitting reading at home, on the bus, at school, just like that, a sudden shortage of oxygen. It terrifies me because there's nothing I can do. The shrink says it's not uncommon at her age, growing pains, he says, that will pass. I ask her what she's anxious *about*, and she doesn't seem to understand. Nothing, she says. Well, she looks fine and is doing well at school, all normal apart from this strange business that just comes on suddenly and leaves her so helpless. They've got her on mild tranquilizers. I know what you'd say, but they say do it so we're doing it. Please don't think it has anything to do with you and me three years ago. She's been fine a long time now."

To further reassure him, Maggie sent a recent photo of Karen at school, surrounded by friends and looking straight at the camera. To Zach, she looked younger than the others in the picture, shyer, brown-eyed, and uncertain.

It started to make him nervous that she was in New York, for all the usual reasons. He began to feel the way he had once in the subway watching a blind saxophonist make his way down one end of the express car, trying to play over the whir of fans and the track noise when the doors between cars flew open. Watching, like everyone else, with that peripheral subway vision (I wa'nt staring at anybody, mister) he followed him slowly up the center aisle, past the drugged latinos blaring transistorized *salsa*, heading straight towards the one really unstable element in the crowd, the brown man in black string-vest and satin shorts, jumping and jiggling his legs, fiddling with a handful of keys and a pocket knife, looking in the heat as if he could blow any minute, vibrating something evil all the way from his black socks and shoes to his crimped fiery red hair.

How was it possible for children to have anxiety attacks? Begin life on tranquilizers? She was a tough child, his daughter, tougher it seemed to him most of the time than he was. She had never cried much as a little girl, or been sick or even much confused. She had been understanding about the divorce, consolatory on her visits to him, full of a touching sympathy that made him feel foolish. She would sit with him, watching out of a corner of an eye to gauge how he "really" was. She inspected his fridge and gave him lectures on nutrition. Before she arrived he'd have to stock up on milk and vegetables, take out the laundry, get rid of the empties. In that respect she had been good for him. He was at a loss now as to how to be good for her. He had thought his absence might be that, a stream of cheerful postcards and winning letters in place of the real thing: the troubled dad, floundering, disconnected. Perhaps she wasn't fooled.

He'd found it harder and harder to accept the terms of her upbringing: that conventional private school his mother paid for, where she palled around with kids of bankers and lawyers, dreamed of assaults laid on hearts of future bankers, lawyers. Having an actress for a mother was prestigious for her—so much he knew, remembered from the eager little faces she used to bring home, introduce to Maggie, but *his* career, that had never been much to set beside the benefits accrued from real fathers: the expensive clothes and vacations, private phones. Not to mention the easy answers. And yet they couldn't send her anywhere else and expect her to get taught, except how to be afraid of her own city and of people her own age. There seemed to be no New York model between these two: the conventional rich and the criminal poor, nothing to help Karen make her own way into her own world. Or was it his world he was talking about: the shaky self-employed and defiant, those who ask questions and those who come unstuck?

Maggie would want her to be a brave child, a young amazon, fearless, honorable, standing on principle and standing alone. Zach wanted these things, but more selfishly, and contradictorily, wanted her to be safe and happy.

And that was no longer (if it ever had been) in his power to control. He had agreed, slowly over the past three years, to drop the interfering, protecting hand, and let her fend for herself in her life with her mother.

Should little girls be spared? Should little girls grow up in cities where there are trees in the squares and the sound of church bells in the evening? Was his little girl going to become a tough little survivor like Rachel, pining for firemen and ambulance sirens, despite her fantastical schooling that contradicted everything she learned on the streets of New York?

And wasn't it possible that some of the horror of the place was not merely that but something akin to magic, too? He remembered riding with her on the lower Broadway bus, the time that other blind man came upon them, slowly mounting the steps of the bus with his dog, becoming more and more visible. In the back someone had sucked air through his teeth—that New York thought: it's going to be bad. The bus was so empty they'd had to see. A real Halloween monster. A teen-age giant in suit and tie. Nearly seven feet tall, white as a sheet and heavy. But his face: in profile it broke in the middle as though the clay had been smashed. His brown eyes were smeared, the lids drawn haywire. And he had no nose: those were holes above his mouth.

A drunk sitting up front, addressing the crowd, denouncing the government, refused to give up his seat, the one reserved for the lame and elderly. Behind him the giant staggered and loomed, while, unaware, he ranted at the ladies who'd quickly signaled him to move and then cut off, and were now pretending in that patient way of public victims that none of this was happening. The giant began to sit, slowly lowering himself from his massive height, and the drunk shifted, still objecting to the request, not knowing that he *had* moved, or for whom, or how nearly he'd been crushed.

Seated, and as though deaf, too, the blind man spoke politely to the driver. Whenever the drunk drew breath you could hear his voice as it came from the lopsided mouth, a slow droning like a record played at the wrong speed. Yet it had dignity. Speaking thus he patted his dog, stared ahead. And the dog, a lovely blond Labrador, gazed into the pulpy face with a mother's eyes: my pride, my beauty.

Perhaps no one wanted the drunk to stop, out of a general fear that he might turn and see what he was sitting with, faint, scream, or turn on the monster in his delirium. But he left the bus, still muttering at the women who had asked him to move, still blind to his blind neighbor. And though the giant was still there with them, the tension in the crowd subsided. Someone made a joke at the drunk's expense, the everyday remark, "It takes all kinds." And it certainly seemed to, because once the anger at thwarted decency had been expressed, followed by a Christian reminder that the drunk could not help himself, once all this was off the chest, and despite the horrific presence still towering over them, the busload relaxed and redefined itself as united, ordinary. The shocks absorbed, they were all once more trundling home-ward, the beautiful dog and the Halloween monster, the helpful ladies and Zach and Karen, all safe, all part of the whole.

He never could explain the force of such episodes nor

ever quite unpeel their mystery. He was often witness to such things in the city, alarmed, uncertainly moved, as he imagined Karen must be, too, by some quality of humanity aroused, provoked by constant violations of the ordinary.

And perhaps it was this that made her anxious, not the division of her parents, but that other division, between what you see and what you're asked to believe. The city was full of cracks that let through an eerie light, laced with menace. But you turned your back at a certain cost. Zach said to himself that Karen would be all right if she kept on looking, and sometime found the courage to acknowledge what she saw.

Zach sat, with his raincoat on his knees, on a low leather sofa where the receptionist put him, and watched his brother around the corner of a doorway, pacing by the side of his desk, talking to a phone with flashing lights. A teen-age girl with green hair slouched in a chair next to him, notepad in one hand, a cigarette in the other, rubbed her eyes, and yawned. Michael, waistcoat unbuttoned, forehead flushed, shouted angrily down the phone, paused, looked cunning, spoke sharply, laughed good-naturedly, winked at his secretary, examined his nails. In and out of their offices women with glossy legs and lips sauntered and perched, glimmered and giggled. Framed ads showed women's mouths around cars and containers. Expensive plant life trembled when the phones rang, thick carpeting sank and rebounded as people found their coats and went to lunch. Outside the windows, clouds glided gently over the distant dome of St. Paul's. Zach sat quietly, feeling himself detached, jobless. But it was not envy. Zach's academic workplace had been funereally somber and he had a memory of dying there.

Michael came down the hallway trailed by the girl with green hair. From his standing position he examined Zach and turned to his companion. "Sara, this is my brother Zachariah," he said. He waited as though expecting laughter. Zach stood. "This is my secretary, Sara Ornley-Scott, a deb in another era, a punk in this."

Sara studied the carpet, she'd heard this before. She accepted the hand Zach held out to her, mumbled, waited for him to put it away.

"OK if Sara comes to lunch?" Michael didn't wait for an answer. He turned to watch a tall blonde make her hipboned approach from the end of the corridor. She took them all in as she walked, slowly, refusing to disturb the languorous roll of hip and slide. She wore loose, soft clothing, bounced upon by extravagant locks. Reaching them, she raised eyes from beyond and smiled.

"Howdy, Miss Howard."

Her mouth made a sultry stretch towards the polished cheeks. She stared at them, waiting.

"My brother Zach," Michael said. She held out a hand which Zach took quickly as though to steady her. "Vanessa," Michael explained.

They rode down in the elevator. "Nice office," Zach said.

"I'll show you around later, first we'll get these girls fed."

Michael led the way out of the elevator and on to the street, pulling Zach along, letting the women trail behind. For two blocks men wearing bowler hats walked without embarrassment.

They entered an Italian restaurant through double glass doors. The carpet business had done well in this part of town, and the chrome merchants. There was a pleasant muted clack and chink of people eating. Sara Ornley-Scott perked up in the surroundings, Ms. Howard barely registered them.

On his way to a window table, Michael nodded left and right. Campari sodas reflected ruby lights onto pink tablecloths. Large men in imperiled jackets mopped plates of garlic and butter, spluttered and spat, wiped their chins, perused the trolleys of desserts.

They sat—Vanessa reluctantly, theatrically, Sara heavily—and took up menus. Vanessa hummed.

Michael dropped his head, smoothed his hair back with both hands; between his wrists his face registered momentary fatigue. He looked up at Zach and winked.

"So what have you been up to this morning?"

"Bought some tangerines," Zach said.

"Another busy day. How're the student digs?"

Vanessa sighed and shifted.

"OK, girls, what are we having?"

They ordered. "Chicken *sorpresa* for the unsurprisable Ornley-Scott," Michael began. Vanessa interrupted him, and addressed the waiter in perfect Italian.

"Make that two," Michael said. He stayed on top.

"Not drinking, Vanessa?"

"I never drink at lunch," she said, patiently, instructively. A soft inhalation of air, a long exhalation, "and today I have the most horrendous hangover."

"Hair of the dog," Michael suggested.

"No, thank you."

"So Sara, tell Zach about your brother's wedding," Michael said and proceeded to tell himself. "Three private planes, two members of the Stones, twelve drug arrests, one unwanted pregnancy, is that right?"

"Yeah," Sara said, "Keith and Charlie."

"Two of the best families in England. A marriage made in heaven, celebrated in jail." Vanessa caught Zach's eye: *not* the very best families evidently.

"Sounds like a lot of fun," Zach said. Sara looked at her green nails, replaced her hands in her lap.

"Sara came to us last summer after school," Michael said. "She speaks three languages. Ask her."

Zach asked her.

"French and German."

"We're still working on the English," Michael said, "not a big talker, our Sara."

Vanessa sighed loudly, found a cigarette, put it between red lips. She waited till Zach found a light for her.

"Thanks," she said. "That's the nicest thing Americans do."

"Lighting cigarettes?"

"Yes. Also car doors, opening them."

"Vanessa's been with us five years," Michael said, "our whiz kid."

"Hardly a kid," Vanessa drawled.

"What do you do?" Zach asked her.

"Oh, this and that."

"I see."

The main course arrived. Sara stabbed the chicken with her fork and watched the butter bleed onto the plate. She ate with preoccupation, her fork in her left hand, her knife in her right, head bent over it.

Vanessa, by contrast, ate deftly with a single fork, entwining green lines of pasta into art nouveau undulations. She kept a cigarette burning in the ashtray beside her; its curling smokerise made consistent idiom with her meal.

"That's enough," she said in a nanny voice to herself. She rubbed her midriff and picked up the cigarette. "Enough, enough. Well Zach," she said, "how long are you staying in London?"

"I'm on no schedule."

"So why go back? What's in New York?"

"Have you been there?"

"Of course. So noisy and self-absorbed. Everyone so tiresomely self-improving."

"That's just a fashion," Michael said.

"Yes," Vanessa said, "like herpes."

"Mickey!" A portly patron loomed towards them beaming. "Mickey, old fart, that Pfeiser's campaign—pure magic. Congrats to you and yours."

"Heh-heh," Michael said, and swiveled his chair to avoid introductions.

"Good reach, good frequency," he said.

"What I most admired," the jowls ingratiated, "was how you rescued the corpse on the storyboard."

"Sure," Michael said, "give them music, you forget there's nothing there."

"Magic," Pinky said again, "something out of nothing: 'A Bottle of Bliss' indeed."

"The client was comfortable with it," Michael said smugly, "rather comfortable." They tilted, laughing, into one another, Pinky bowing, weaving, hesitating, sauntering off.

"Larry Kershaw," Michael said to Vanessa, "one of the old school."

"Where is he now?"

"Judd and Cronin."

"Oh dear, who will outlast whom I wonder?" She tossed her locks behind her.

"Neither," Michael said, "sooner or later they'll go and so will Larry. Trick about this business," he lectured them briefly, "is to keep it fresh as tomorrow."

"So you always say."

"A real Willy Loman," Michael said to Zach, "rides on a smile and a shoeshine."

"Spot on his hat," Vanessa quoted, "and he's through."

"Pretty ruthless business, eh?" Zach said to them.

"And we got it from you," Vanessa smiled at him, leaned towards him, and sat back.

"Not from Zach," Michael told her, "Zach's something of a renegade Yank, culture don't-you-know, music."

"Music, still?" Vanessa asked.

"Not rock music."

"Oh, avant-garde, I suppose. Nothing I follow."

"Nothing Zach pursues, *very* avant-garde, entirely conceptual. Sing us a few bars, Zach, of your latest."

Zach sat a while in silence, coupled now with Sara; resentment vapored from both.

"Seriously, did you find a piano?"

"For imaginary music?" Vanessa flirted with him, waited, changed attack and turned on Michael: "What happened to the talent with you?"

"Burned out at thirty, as is proper."

After coffee, and simultaneously, the women rose and moved toward the rear of the restaurant.

"So how do you like the girls?" Michael demanded.

"Which one did you figure was mine?"

"Why are you so irritated? You always forget I love you."

"I always do."

"You like Vanessa?"

"In what capacity exactly?"

"Name it."

"Pretty generous, Michael, breaking up the harem like this. I'm touched, but I have my own plans, thanks."

"Oh yes, and how are we progressing?"

"What is it about you and Anne?"

"Me and Anne? It's you I worry about. You're just not being careful."

"That's your wisdom, eh, be careful. That's it. That's the whole wisdom?"

"And yours? What virtue do you imagine you possess and I don't, what freedom apart from the freedom to fall on your ass, hitch up with more disaster, walk into the mine-fields yet again? You're only prolonging your adolescence, Zach, with this patriotic but infantile pursuit. Face it, brother, the world is no longer your oyster. Never was. There are things you ought to be doing."

"Things like this?"

"And things, people, you ought not."

"Such as Anne?"

"Such as Anne, right now, yes."

"Say good-bye to the ladies," Zach said, "the game doesn't interest me. I'm off." He slapped a twenty-pound note on the table.

"Don't insult me," Michael said, handing back the note. "You still need me."

"I don't need this," he indicated the place, the direction in which the women had disappeared. "I'll catch you later," he said, "when you're a little less the public man." Nodding in mock politeness to the headwaiter, he exited through the glass doors, and hailed a cab out on the street.

They passed the opening of a park and Zach got out. He walked across muddy ruts where horses had been, across open lawns cut by arterial slate paths. Elderly women and short-haired terriers assessed him without approval. He noticed his disruptive gait: he was stomping. Over the uneven ground he lost his footing and swayed. They must have thought him drunk.

He found his brother absurd, as absurd as his women, and it hurt him to realize this was so. He imagined wildly he should save him, blow the smug little world apart with a blast . . . of what? New York anarchic life? Michael's commitments bound him here. Let him enjoy his costume party then. He was keeping others happy.

To be free meant to be tortured and ridiculous. He sat now among the unemployed, the plotting young, and wandering Arabs, and sadly contemplated the duck life on the pond before him. He had made a fool of himself leaving the restaurant. He had not waited to be shown around the office. He had declared superiority and hurt his brother's feelings. He was sad now and lost. What was he up to, snorting and refusing the terribly little that was asked of him: a marginal man in a marginal life, banging on the margins and asking for entry, refusing to enter as soon as the invitation lay in his hand?

Slowly he registered the life around him: the quarreling and industry of the ducks, the bench maneuvers of the old and stately, the furtive sexual glancing of the young. Everyone was busy. His own distress lifted and wafted away. He sat there emptily, strung between boredom and sadness. A stiff, half-peeled stick lay by his feet on the ground. He lifted it, fingered the bark and the green, let his hand close over it and take its weight. He let his feelings disperse and at the same time tapped with the stick on a bar of the bench a tune of those feelings. Tip, tip, tip, he began, pianoless on his bench in the park, tapping the stick now against his notebook, smoothing out its pages, humming, beginning to write it down: an aleatory music like his life, proceeding along a line that strung the most banal of incidents above a wave of feelings: love arguing with confusion, his love for his life, his confused love for all of them. I know too much, he said, I stutter. Tip, tip, tip, this was what he was here for, a strange contentment as he beat out the line, as though at last he was doing what he was meant to: nothing more than recording his feelings. Self-consciousness now and a clue: Art must proceed, he told himself, like his life, from freedom to necessity, from a beginning where everything is possible to the point where only one thing is right, from can to must, to yes through no. And then another thing, his art and his life must all be one and the same. And how is that? Zach addressed himself aloud now on the bench among the citizens and Mussulmen, bathed in the pink of the evening: the small necessity, the small thing you know. From this, both work and love, no, work about love, work as love. What was it Maggie wrote about artists saving it? Well, he would live it and write it both, fuse them, of necessity. And furthermore, the task was to make out of the utterly formless energies of sensation and emotion something you can bring out again, something as simple as a melody.

But was it any good, the work or the life? He poised his silver pencil and pondered. Another question entirely. Surrender, let it go, put all that in the hands of others. Your job, Zach, is to hum. Moment, moment, he reminded himself, it's so easy to be happy.

Feeling broke through narrative as Zach made his notations, heard the musical incidents as thin cover for the spirit inside. Yes, yes, I get it, Zach muttered, but what is it for? Not for anything but itself. A small witness to the present. He let his imaginary music take him back, create a complex machine of instrumental bleat and declaration, until mocking, still consoling, the music ran itself to silence and then broke apart, gave way inside his head to a small choral finale, so that in place of honor and high above the questioning brass, he heard, plaintive, heroic, living, erotic, the triumphant comfort of the human voice.

Two contrary movements, like a kind of music, his and Anne's. His desire insistent, repeating, to push further and further towards her, own and possess her utterly; hers to step away, camouflage and flee. The Englishness was at her service, the play and skip on the surface, the evasive phrases and moves that could make an evening an act of juggling, until Zach stepped in, silently, like the cowboy in a Marlboro ad, removed the props, stilled her, and took her over. He found the game hypnotic, intoxicating, like a snake with a rabbit.

He saw in their sexual dance a difference between their cultures, geography, and history: the traditional America conceived of as an alien environment, what you pit your wits and courage against, and the England that cradled, looked after, and engulfed you. Hence in England, the tradition of the seafarer, empire-builder; the heroism of escape. Hence in America, the tradition of frontiersman and pioneer, journeying deeper and deeper into the body of the continent. Not flight from the familiar as in England, but towards Oedipal possession: the mysterious mother country.

Anne's skitteriness, independence, was the English form: easy to be outlandish if the land is there behind you, waving its hankie, wishing you bon voyage, assuring its continuity on your return. In New York, if you turn your head, whole sections are likely to disappear. No wonder the characteristic move was the greedy sprint, that or the stumbling, shell-shocked, bag-lady shuffle, plastered and bloody, sifting through the rubble, clutching the remains. From Marlboro man to derelict, Zach with Anne had a broadswept and historical American role. Epic, he would say, next to her comedy of manners.

She was an infuriating lover. She gave him the keys to her flat and was never there. She went about like a debutante, with six closets full of clothes to rush around in. She knew too many people and not enough, and none of them made her happy. She wouldn't let him make her happy. She didn't stop that long. And yet he thought he loved her. They slept together and sometimes went out together, and that was how it progressed, along a tense courteous continuum that could not climb and had not yet descended.

The women truly baffled him. He couldn't make out what they wanted. He couldn't figure out what propelled Anne's life and where its satisfactions lay. He had never understood what Maggie wanted from her uneasy freedom. Or Rachel, spurning Bloomsbury for the thrill of what you'd see in a TV ad for beer. Some hand had wound them up and set them on the pavement to charge along like toy mice. No one wanted to sit still anymore, except Helen, of course, still and no less mysterious.

What was it you were supposed to want? Something other than this, surely, the heedless pursuit. Or was it flight? There were days when it was hard to distinguish one from the other.

"Why won't you take me to this party?" he asked her.

"I can't, Zach. Don't press me. It wouldn't work."

"Work? I'll wear a suit. I'll tell no jokes. I won't embarrass you."

"I go to parties alone. I told you that. Why do you even want to come?" She tossed her head at him, caught between the charming gesture and adamant refusal. They verged on fighting, she pretended it wasn't serious.

"There's something wrong with this," he said. "Are you ashamed?"

"Of course not."

"How else do I read it?"

"Not of you. Perhaps it's the other way around. Do you ever think? Perhaps you'll see my life as empty."

"Would I?"

"Like yours? Don't force things, Zach. Let me have my frivolous existence safe from your scrutiny. I don't question your ponderous self-examinations in London. You don't hear me demanding you become serious."

"What would be serious?"

"Going home."

"But I'm not going home. I've told you that. It's elsewhere I want to go. With you. I'm here with you." He took her hand and she let him hold it.

"The mythical Elsewhere," she said. "It's not at the bloody party. Coming with me won't change anything. My privacy, that's all. We're too old, too wise, even, to do this to one another. Just take what's offered."

"And is it enough for you? Honestly?"

She didn't answer him.

"You can't crash through into something solid if it's not there," she said finally. "I've told you that. You can't lean on me, I'm not reliable."

"Then make yourself," Zach said.

"And you," Anne asked him, "how reliable are you?"

When she came out, dressed for her party, she looked at him, docilely reading in her white armchair. "I won't be long," she said. "Will you be here when I get back?"

"Yes," he said, "I've just told you that."

She sat down next to him on the arm of the chair. "I might as well tell you that Helen seems to think I'm in some spiritual danger involving myself with you. 'At least he's not married,' I said, and she said, 'Ah, but he is.' If you scratch Helen's indifference you come up against an almost Catholic sensibility. Once is forever, she thinks, when the truth is once is sometimes hardly anything. I was hardly married to Sam, which may be why we can still be friends. Perhaps Helen's feelings explain a lot about her and Michael, which I never understand, how she can just get lost in that life of theirs, sunk without a trace. Well, other people's marriages. The Catholic view is right in one respect, it certainly is a mystery.

"And this with you is a little mystery, with a farcical element—you trying to disentangle me from my life here, my husbands, my parties, when your own webbing is so tight. You think it's all a question of your courage, but you haven't a clue how much it would take for me to leap my bounds, frolic with such a bad proposition. No, the frolic's not the problem, it's the taking seriously. Have I still got it in me? And if I haven't? And if this shows me I haven't? What conclusion then? What am I holding out for? Half the time I'm not sure it's still there, not just for me, for anyone."

"A new nightclub," she said to him, coming in late that evening. "They had a Gypsy palm-reader there, but it was so dark she had to use a torch. That's funny, isn't it, to have a fortune-teller in a nightclub so she can't see a thing?"

"And you've been all this time getting your fortune told? It's two A.M. Anne, you've got a long life."

"She said I should think of my life as a blanket with moth holes, she said the more holes there are the more you can see into the real world where it all makes sense. She was telling me all this in the dark over a hell of a lot of noise. I'm not sure I got it exactly. Moth holes, yes. She said I drank too much, not brilliant, you say, but I was dead sober at the time. She said I didn't have to drink because the holes are there anyway and all I have to do is look for them.

She said I drank in order to shred the blanket. What about that theory, eh?"

She was in her confrontational mode, her legs straight out in front of her on a facing chair. She had a drink in her hand and her coat on the floor. She knew she was desirable. He could see she'd been told that all night.

"What else?" Zach said.

"She said I was a great actress. I said I was a jewelry designer, she said I was an actress nevertheless. Your wife is, isn't she?"

"Yes."

"Is she like me?"

"No. What else?"

"Well, my dear, she said I had had my big love and another wasn't coming for some time. She said I'd have to learn to be myself before it did, not to be afraid of myself because I was all right. She said God was on my side but I didn't believe it, thought it was Him against me. I said, Who is God? She said I was and she was, and that He was with us while she read my palm with her pocket torch. She said I kept losing Him/It all the time. I said God was an invention. She said yes, of a particular kind. We are all orphans, she said, and in God we reinvent our parents."

"Pretty holy woman for a nightclub. What else?"

"I asked about us, you and me. Not going to work out, she said. 'Sometimes people are not given to each other,' she said, 'so that they will have to turn to God instead.' "

"And you listened to all this till two A.M.? Did she say anything that made sense?"

"She said I used to live in a hot country and I would again."

"Did you?"

"I lived in Cairo for two years with Adrian."

"Anything else?"

"Go to the dentist, she said."

Sometimes he would read till she fell asleep. Then he would lay the book down and watch her in the half-light that his lamp extended, casting shadows over her shoulders and throat, burrowing into her hair, wheat-colored, bronzed, as though she were a creature of the sun. Asleep, she crawled away from his arm, further into the shadow on her side of the bed. He would pick up his book again and listen to her breathing in the darkness.

The door of the bedroom gave on to the hallway and beyond that to the door of the big room, left open so that the cat could wander. This night it sat between them at the foot of the bed, unnaturally alert, watching Zach as he read, getting up to look at Anne. He turned off the light and slept. Waking again in the darkness, he saw the cat across the room, sitting up and listening, as he began to listen to the noises Anne was making beside him, a breathless sound like someone sobbing, and a kind of growling low in the throat. Something drew his attention to the large room beyond the doors. In the darkness he saw faint light near the windows, a street reflection. Only it wasn't that. He touched his face, he was sweating. His shirt was wet. Her body was shaking, but he did not wake her, could not. For several minutes he was frozen listening to sounds that were barely human.

She sat up suddenly in her sleep: "It is over," she said.

He woke her then, shaking her gently. She seemed dazed, and utterly peaceful.

"What is over?" he asked her. "What was the dream?"

"I'll go," she said when he told her, "I'm not afraid," like a mother might say it, happy to challenge the darkness. He watched her cross the hallway, certain that what he felt had not yet left. He tried to call her back but could not speak.

"There's nothing here."

"But there was," he said. He tried to describe it.

"Then I'm free," she said, "if it's over. I've been exorcised. Thank God," she said, "if that's what it was."

In the morning she pretended it had only been Zach's imagination.

"Exorcised of what?" he demanded.

"You misunderstood." She tried to laugh at him. She refused to discuss it again. But later, once, she said, "Who knows, Zach, perhaps it really is over."

One night, sleeping next to Anne, he dreamed fitfully a dream of himself banging like a moth against a lamplit window, while inside Maggie and Karen talked without him. A man now, he knocked at the door, a suitcase by his feet. It was his mother who opened it to him. A boy now, he pushed past her in the hallway and ran to embrace his wife and daughter. They shouted when they saw him, got up and fled the room. His mother motioned him to a chair, sat facing him, began to cry. He rose, searched the house for his family, but when he entered the room, they did not see him. He took off his clothes and got into bed next to them. Maggie rolled over, embracing her daughter, lifting her, a baby, high in the air. Zach took up no space in the bed. They could not hear him.

They sat in sweaters in her garden, holding cups of tea, holding conversation. A bough swung in the breeze so that leaves fluttered and fell under their wicker chairs, up against the flower beds, still green, onto a rubber ball the cat had played with and abandoned. The two boys came crashing out of doors, passed, touched their mother, ran in again, shouting up the stairs and out of the windows until, meeting no resistance, they stopped and played quietly in an upstairs room.

Zach alone with Helen in her garden, fought the peace that fell upon them, squirmed against the formality much as he'd done as a schoolboy called in for questioning, subtly tortured under framed portraits of school presidents, overpowered by the sudden carpeting and china of the head's study, out of his element of yellow wooden desks and muddy fields and the savage codes of prep school. Only now he was the interviewer, the Yankee questioner as she made him aware, something like the bull in the shop, asking so di-

rectly. She didn't balk, nor quite evade, but more cleverly—
if indeed it was conscious—she turned his questions round
and emptied them of meaning, so that by the sounds of
things at least, they were simply chatting away affably on
topics pleasant, improving to them both.

Yet it was pain that had brought him there, and his sense
of mystification. And here was more mystification, as though
they were both saying nothing for fear of the anger. So he
returned again and again to the questions, until he said
finally: "Yes, but Helen, this doesn't explain it."

Sometimes he was aware how much he resented them,
their superior knowledge of the spiritual, the broody soli-
tudes and possession of the mysteries. As condescending
and protective as his mother had been once school had
separated them, doling out the truth in boy-manageable
portions. Likewise, Helen hardly trusted him with answers.
Like Maggie announcing her departure. A mere casually
executed formality to let him know why. He asked again,
woodenly, like the caricature American she forced him to
be: What is it about Anne that makes her stop? What is it
about Anne and Michael? What was it that happened between you that so cripples the present?

But there's no past to uncover, she said, and Anne's my
greatest friend, and You mustn't mind Michael.

"Well, all right then," she said, "it was nothing really,
only this, a kind of theological dispute perhaps, a philo-
sophical divergence, having to do with happiness and how
it's got and at what cost, and then a small, unimportant
now, but once important minor flight—of mine—and per-

haps Michael's memory of all that. If he sees Anne as a threat to peace, then it's his peace, not yours. Perhaps because he cannot distrust me, he distrusts her. Misplaced aggression, I believe may be the term.

"It seems so long ago now, and nothing to do with the present, nor am I sure that that's the problem if there is one between you and Anne or you and Michael, but all right, I will tell you and you can make of it what you will. Let me just check that the boys are all right."

So she left him in the garden and made the noises of a purposeful joyous motherhood upstairs, grating on his nerves and making him wait until she sat down again and threw out at him somewhat in anger: "The only thing I can think you think you want to know is something that happened years ago. I needn't tell you, Zach, that it's awkward only because of Michael. He'd be mortified that we were talking about this or that you knew. I mean if he were English it would be very different I think, God knows in our set it's happened many times, oh, many things happen that I don't get the impression happen in America or at least not without consequence, I mean women going off. Here it's almost *de rigueur*, and of course men going off. The Clarkes, for example, whom you met the other night, even the mistress comes to dinner, and occasionally with a lover. I mean sometimes, Zach, it doesn't feel very grown-up that American way, because after all life doesn't stop after marriage, does it? Though of course sometimes that's precisely what happens. You and Maggie, were you always so happy? I think, you see, the feeling here is that divorce may be the worst thing, if there are children, and so people accommodate. I suppose that could seem shocking, well if you're like Michael, he really is the most old-fashioned. It can get oppressive . . . sometimes. Not, I will tell you, that I did anything in that way. But I know that if I had and if Michael had known, then that would have been it, the boys notwithstanding. Divorce. Truth to feeling, isn't it, a little arrogant, isn't it, self-righteous, puritan?"

"Yes, perhaps," Zach said.

"Well, all I did—it's hard now to remember why, when now I do really feel content. Or maybe I've just stopped shaking the world and demanding things it cannot give, resigned maybe, middle-aged maybe, but nonetheless content for that, for not hauling out my feelings every bloody morning and asking, am I happy, is it enough? Well, it just is, you get on with it, don't you, and then it either is OK or it's not, but does it matter so very much after all? There are other people to be considered. All I did was leave, very briefly, inconsequentially, and stay with Anne to try and find out what Anne knew.

"I see you think I'm telling you that I'm *not* happy, that I'm just being brave. But the truth is I really have been very happy with Michael ever since I came back to him and decided really to throw out the question rather than the life. Anyway, you want to know about Anne, not me, and the thing is she isn't like that, because to her I think—and that is why I admire her as much as I'm afraid for her—to her it's not a question of happiness, despite the life she lives, which everyone assumes to be out of some sort of shallow

149

hedonism, not about happiness but something harder to describe. I can only use the word correctness, a sort of ethical thing, that doesn't let her stop where it isn't right, and therefore doesn't let her stop at all. Hence her wild and awful mistakes, hence the extremity of the rituals, those two bloodletting marriages, and then the wildly mourned death of her first husband—"

Here Zach interrupted. "Death? She never said, no one said, divorce, I thought."

"No, it was death, mourned to the point of taking death upon herself for all of two years, fueled by drink and a frenzied round of parties. Anne goes to parties and into affairs like some glory-driven matador. And who knows what she's looking for—some mystery buried inside the platitudes of normal social life—who knows except the rare men that sense it and respond, or the wives that shun her. And for the past few years she's lived like this, half-understood, frequently mocked, though generally accorded some sort of survivor's gumption. Well, I think a few people did know what was behind that search, Sam for instance, though he was helpless against her willful isolation—and maybe myself.

"And now I'm no longer sure about this bravery of Anne's and what it's for, and whether the mystery and correctness might not be got in more marginal ways, not sucked out but simply derived from the ordinary doings of daily life."

She seemed to have finished on this note of doubtful assertion. They sat in silence for a while, Zach revising his sense of Helen and of Anne in the light of this strangely concealed fact of her first husband's death.

"I have to tell you, Zach, that in the years since I returned to Michael and the boys, after my few months away, the subject of my escape has never been discussed between us, except in the first few days of my return, just as it was never discussed between Michael and Anne. It has simply disappeared as a part of history, detached from present consequences, more or less disregarded in questions of motivation and procedure. My continued friendship with Anne, Michael accepts as you know with poor grace, a kind of bad sportsmanship in the circumstances, but otherwise it hardly impinges on our lives together. No shadow, as far as I know, fell on the boys, either. What it has affected is my relation to Anne, because I no longer feel morally able to share her life by asking or giving advice. I think my return appeared to Anne—and I've found it too hard and too demeaning to try to separate appearance from reality—as an act of cowardice, a shameful shuffle back to where things were simply comfortable. I think Anne saw it that way and forgave me for it, knowing her own mission to be headstrong if not simply masochistic. She's no proselytizer Anne, never—contrary to Michael's suspicions—encouraged the move or delayed the return. She was simply there, then, with the spare bed and the set of keys and a lot of listening. And I know that my present contentment must be mysterious to her, and for that reason feel and have felt for the last three years a constraint in talking about such matters, as though our apparent equality would seem presumptuous.

"So anyway, I'm rather out of things, cordoned off to the sidelines of those whose souls aren't so serious as to participate in the great struggle, but Michael doesn't know that, fears that Anne is still some kind of siren for me, for the spiritual adventure—though he pretends her adventure's merely physical. And you, too, perhaps you seem something of a potential siren to him: your freedom, the other side of your distress. Well, together, you and Anne, positively whores of Babylon, spiritually speaking. He assumes I feel tamed by my life with him and the boys. Well, I *am* tamed, by the conviction that you can be content, I mean genuinely so, if you only give up the death squeeze on the whole issue."

"But once you were not content," Zach said, and his pain now shifted. He was sad for his brother, who played so little part in this woman's happiness, who seemed so foolish to them both, in Helen's word "spiritually" (at the very least) cuckolded. The abandoned brothers. For a moment he saw them that way. Except that this wife had come back, if only in body. She sat in his brother's garden, explaining, as he had asked her. Irritation crept upon him.

"Yes, once. For a few months I left your brother and my children to stay with Anne, to find something I never found. Am I to be punished forever? But then, really, I was never punished.

"But now, let me ask you," she said. "How serious are you about Anne, and what can you offer her, in transit like this? Do you think about it even? And Karen, and your whole life back there? Are you even over Maggie? I liked Maggie," she said, "it was a pity all that."

Zach pushed open the white lacquered door of Anne's flat, dark and empty except where the neon sign of a Greek restaurant flashed erratically through the trees of the garden square, casting shadows through Anne's long, heavy windows, onto the dirty white carpet and the corner of the high cat-battered armchair, as each colored letter lit on the beat, halfhearted, irregular, pink, yellow, green, green, pink, yellow, yellow. He switched on the lamp and the colors stopped, but not the sounds or smells that for Zach gave the place its Englishness, a peculiar relation to water: internal sounds of plumbing and tea making, whistling kettles and groaning pipes, the odor of faint mildew and damp plastering. A late October mist that was both fog and frost fell in soft light on the littered grass and thinning trees outside. In America the autumn frosts would have arrived by now, dramatically ravishing the trees, blasting the leaves with garish color, vulgarly announcing the fall.

The flat was dusty and bare. He hadn't noticed this before.

When they were together her presence stirred the room with liveliness. He thought it beautiful with its high rose-plastered ceiling and tall gray mantel where the invitations lay spread: At Home, they said, so and so At Home, At Home to Anne, Not At Home to Zach.

He removed his shoes and pushed the cat off its chair so that he could watch the neon and wait for Anne to return. The cat fell on its feet and began to rub against his trousers, sinking its claws into the fabric in little erotic pummelings, sidling against his shins until Zach pushed it away. Two nights ago it had dragged a wounded bird from the terrace and tortured it slowly while Anne and Zach lay sleeping. During the night Zach had heard its sexual chirping as it worked, and a soft continuous bumping against the bottom corner of the mattress, as though a child were beating a rag doll. In the morning he had found the empty thorax cavity of the bird with its wings still spread like a crucifixion, then the open-beaked, black-eyed head five yards beyond. With a brush and pan he had rolled the skull and lifted the awkward body, flopping, from the floor. The feathers were now still scattered in the corners of the bedroom among the red seeds and dried corn it had eaten. Anne, waking, had cried watching Zach pick up the clawed feet, still attached to the black feathered pantaloons.

Once with Maggie there had been an infestation of mice. He had set out traps and waited. He had put out pellets of poison and waited. Then he had bought the little cardboard trap-houses whose floors were spread with glue. Practicing on the Steinway one afternoon, he had heard between the notes a high crying noise coming from the kitchen. He had not believed mice could sound so human, but when he crouched over the traps, painted crudely with latticed windows and a suburban red door, he saw them inside, three infant squeaking mice stuck by paws and tail, facing East, West, and South, their hearts banging visibly inside their straw ribs. For hours they'd cried while Zach tried to master the situation. At the last minute, just before Karen was due back from school, he had opened the windows and thrown the boxes out, letting the mice sail out into space, glued on all fours, tails protruding in the wind. After that he had let the mice run rampant in the kitchen. It had been Maggie finally who got the exterminator.

Anne's jewelry-making tools were out of their cases and on the table. Beside them were the lumps of blue and red stones she would polish and set later in gold. She must have been working this afternoon. He never saw her at it. She put her things away when he was there. He didn't know how she made her money, or how she fared. The signals were conflicting. It seemed he knew very little about her. He knew her body.

The phone rang in the apartment. The cat stared at him, challenging him to respond. He sat through its ringing, feeling more and more an intruder in their lives. He who had come to ask questions, demand an explanation.

He still had choices, of course. He could visit Dinah, spend the winter in Italy. Or in New York. The picture was there for him, out on the streets: the bitter cold between the downtown blocks, black and white lines of snow against the curbs, embedding trucks and slowing pedestrians, their mouths wrapped against the air, snuffling moisture, stomping booted along, moving along like the cabs, whose wheels jingled in chains, or frozen in traffic, sat steaming over manholes. He thought of that clear winter light: up the pure blue howling around the towers, and down the grays and black, cut by the ribs of rusting fire escapes.

Or he could stay, here where the winter was no winter but a progressive shabbiness of air and sky. Watch his feelings get shabby too, like this room, like the furniture. Certainly. In his wildest thoughts, he could imagine himself ending up like Michael, a misplaced, indulged, joke foreign husband, humored and tricked by the natives. Or not even: "She'll go so far with you and then she'll walk back to where she's safe." (This from Michael.) "It's that reckless sadness she chooses."

What was he to be allowed to do with her exactly? She gave him such little room to maneuver in her life. Sometimes it was clear he was meant to remain marginal, a kind of pick-me-up between parties, a place like a booth for confessions, renewals, a release for frustrations with London, with the trivial, with the aimless wandering it seemed she engaged in no less than he. And yet to her this rootlessness was something fixed, on no account to be disrupted. That Helen should worry abut Anne, the thing was farcical. Both of them monstrous out of conviction of their own vulnerability. Just so far and no further. Both of them. He was sad for his brother, and a little sorry now for himself. But for himself, why did he stay? That large And Yet.

Something not explained, something in her that offered transformation. Rilke's imperative:

"If there weren't light . . .
the body wouldn't send out light from every edge as a star
   does . . .
for there is no place at all that isn't looking at you.
You must change your life."

The medium of New York was solitude. Must he really return to that? Sit in that darkness and make something out of nothing? Be an artist again, exchange life for a few notes, the blinded songbird? Was there no community here that might be less than a dishonest proposition?

Michael. He had last seen Michael bent over his leather sofa, cleaning it with lemon oil and a chamois cloth. Which of them now seemed more foolish?

She came in late. He rose to greet her. Something formal in his manner made her pause. I want to talk to you.

"Oh dear," she said, mocking him. She took off her coat and went to the kitchen and came back with drinks for them both. He took the glass, put it down next to him and sat her near him. I want you to tell me, he said.

"Did you know," she said, "I heard it on the tele, stars are blurs of events that happened years ago." She regarded him coolly. "You want to know about Adrian," she repeated. "You think I kept something from you, calling it a divorce. Well, we did divorce, a year before he died. You want to hear what his death cost me? Is that it? You want to know about the pain?"

"Yes," he said.

"And is that because like Thomas you can only believe if you can stick your hand into the wound? Or is it something else? Something more like lust? You want to hear about suffering. It'll spur you, will it? Whet a jaded appetite?" She laughed at him. "I don't owe you anything."

He hadn't moved in his chair. He drank his drink. She watched him.

"I took care of Adrian, you see. He was a little weak. He drank too much. My own drinking . . . a kind of memorial rite, really, freshens the grave, takes the edge off. He's buried in the mud, you know, deep in the countryside where it always rains. The grave was deep in water when the casket slid in, slopped in so the water sloshed over it, not very dignified. The drinking would have killed him if he hadn't crashed the plane. The doctors told him. He would have died anyway. His liver was shot. At thirty his liver was already shot. Can you imagine?" she said.

"We love people," she said softly, "and it's not enough. Do you understand? No one gets saved. Not by being loved. Not by loving. No one saves anyone. The most, the most you can do . . ." she stopped.

"Tell me," Zach said.

"Ourselves. Or we can try. We can get by, that's all. You can't save me, Zach. Sam couldn't, he tried to lead me like Orpheus out of my mourning. But he couldn't touch me. I was lost for him, under the mud with Adrian. All he could do was leave. And I can't save you, Zach."

"I'm not asking it," he said.

"Oh, aren't you? You would have been impressed by the funeral. Particularly grand, a double funeral, you see. The copilot was Adrian's brother." She waited for him to speak, and then went on. "The funeral was held in a tiny church on the grounds of Adrian's family place, a chapel really. There was hardly room for all the people who wanted to come. There were two aisles down the church, no more than six seats across. People stood at the back. It was raining that day, as I told you, and the church became very dark. There were a lot of candles, and of course a lot of flowers, and I think they put the electric lights on. Still, it was terribly dark, and the flowers were overpowering in that humidity. We sat and listened to the tributes and stared at the coffins that lay side by side taking up all the space there was at the front. I don't think there was much crying, but people fanned themselves with their programs and one way or another breathing was difficult. The tributes went on a long time, almost in defiance of what was overwhelmingly clear, looming over us on the dais. One after another friends, family, spoke, read poems, insisted that these men had been loved, that their lives hadn't merely passed, but that something remained, precious, irrefutable. It was a service of thanksgiving, really, rather than a burial. We were united, stifled, exhilarated by what we were listening to, as though our love could hold them even momentarily away from death or the fact that they were gone. We were convinced by our words, they became more real finally than those massive black boxes, a kind of triumph, as they say, a victory. We were safe as long as anyone spoke, but then that part of things came to an end, and while we were singing the last hymn, all of us standing, there came suddenly through the back of the church what seemed an obscenity. An army of enormous black-suited pallbearers, all local men, farmers with broad shoulders and red faces. I remember their shoes, noisy, heavy, enormous, beetle-crushing shoes, still muddy from the walk to the church. And they were wearing dark cheap pulling suits. I'm sorry, Zach, but that is what I remember, that and the number of them in that tiny space: twelve because there were two coffins. They could barely squeeze through the aisle. When we finished and sat down, they stood in front of us a long terrible time, shuffling on the stone, adjusting their shoulders under the coffins. Then they led the bodies down past us and away. We were left with nothing. We followed them in the rain. They put the coffins in the graves outside. I think the organist played for a while, but the sound of the rain overpowered the music. No one bothered with umbrellas. We just stood there watching the ritual with the mud and coffins feeling empty and helpless and defeated.

"I suppose I held out all those years against that awful burial and the black-suited farmers. I suppose that's what it's been, my own defiance. I suppose I felt as long as I refused to let him go, he would not go, or that somehow I could make up for all that had gone wrong between us. It was a kind of reunion we had, sick maybe, no doubt they said so. Sometimes I would lie awake at night and open my arms to him and I could feel his weight on me. Then little by little I couldn't feel him any longer. I spent a lot of time trying to get him back. A certain stage of drink could do it, or exhaustion. A crack would open, I'd get a glimpse. I lived for those moments. Nothing else even registered. No matter how long it took for us to find each other each time, no matter what humiliations that required. Anyway, into all this poor Sam blundered in his kindly, overbearing way. But it was all too soon. I wasn't ready to give up my— necrophilia. All he ever had of me was a surface. Highly inadequate, wouldn't you say?"

"Orpheus, you called him," Zach said.

"Orpheus, a good name. He's so charming, stray animals follow him home. But I remained under in my underworld. Nothing in this life had remotely the power for me that that darkness had."

"Had?"

"I don't know. I don't know if it's over yet. Or what there's left for me if I do come back. It seems so inadequate, doesn't it, Zach, ordinary life? So demeaning and trivial, doesn't it? Say it. Say it at least so I can hear you tell the truth. That would be something, wouldn't it? To name it at least. Say it isn't enough."

There were Rachel's hairpins in the drawers, Rachel's cereal in the kitchen cupboard, Rachel's few acquaintances on the phone and their messages pushed through the mail slot and lying in the stone hallway waiting for Zach's daily return. Her life in London had dwindled to these few signs that the place had not held her.

For weeks now he had seen nothing of Michael and Helen and little enough of Anne. In the mornings he sat at his hired piano playing other men's music. He practiced a small repertoire, looking for entrance into his own work by way of connection with theirs. Over and over he pushed himself inside their phrasing, squeezing the notes for an understanding of his own life, for a way in, a way out.

The fogbreath of English winter was upon him. Already the sea and sky were fusing, islanding the island. Vapor rose around it like a sea monster, blurry-eyed and gray. Already the street lamps were comforting, and taking tea and the evening smells from the cafes. On the streets, by the shores of large puddles, pigeons hovered in small groups, hunch-shouldered and fretful as the Burghers of Calais. The streets grew soggy as the newspaper kiosks, where commuters, circle-eyed, day-disordered, bought their evening papers as they streamed from work. Still, he stayed, vulnerable to the alien weather, in someone else's damp, using their chipped crockery, forwarding their letters.

When he thought of New York, it was as the place of his past, where he had been young, where he had been in love. He had married a woman and fathered a child and they had both gone on without him. Unbearable sadness that he could not keep up, but had been left behind. Their loss had fractured, not freed, him. There was fear, too, in understanding that.

Anne had shown him both these things: the depth of his grief, mirrored in hers, and the fearful consequences of it. He had pushed her to the truth and she had named it for him. His truth. It was now there in all its clarity, the hold of the past and its cost. The fact was there were only fragments left to give.

It seemed ironic to him that his time with Anne had given him back his love—entirely hopeless and painful—for his wife. His young wife, not the present Maggie, for whom he felt a friendly sympathy, nor the recent Maggie toward whom the bitterness remained, but the woman of his early years, who came back to him now, conceived whole, pure, unmarked, sprung as from the head of a god. It was a curious gift, the image of delight and the response of pain. Crystal clear she was, his young wife, infused with his young life, his best courage. Gone she was, with ground gained, wise, even kinder now, doubtless, but lost to him: the young girl and her daughter. These two had vanished and taken him with them. He felt hollow, left with nothing, nothing to begin over with, or not enough.

He let them go. He blessed them in his mind. He wished them well and more. Still he could not move forward. He retraced his thoughts, trying to break the ties, find his own first footing. If he'd freed them in his mind, why was he still bound? Well, then, he should step forward into his new life. But there, too, Anne, lost to Adrian, stopped him.

Suppose they took each other on? Was there only second best available, the first self spent? What of that notion of adult love as better, stronger, the childishness, egotism, and trauma burnt away? Or was that only because one could never get close again? Intactness because nothing can touch? Only the past touches you, deeply, where you used to be.

Anne's refusal, he saw that now, was his own, an obstinacy in the face of that common sense. Carrying on. No, it was not enough. Honorable, holding out, incorruptible, they would freeze to death.

He said these things to her. She nodded and understood. She even agreed with him how it might be a question simply of trying. In bed the constraints of the old loves slipped away from them, and they inhabited a present that belonged to them alone. But afterward, as the heat left their bodies, the sadness returned, because after all, they had not escaped. The link from body to spirit had yet to be built. The heart like a broken bridge held them back.

Their meetings dwindled with their innocence. He had not seen her for over a week when he heard from her that she was going away. Then came Helen's call, protective, concerned, gentle, and after that, Anne's letter:

I don't know what you will make of this, or of me. You may be right in feeling this a betrayal of everything we've talked about, and perhaps it is. In a way, my decision has something to do with you and our failure. You've made me afraid, that's the truth. Afraid that if I couldn't love you enough to jump into the future, I wouldn't have any future at all, just more of the same.

No, I never gave Sam a chance. You asked me that once, do you remember? And I said, of course I had, but I never did, never got beyond my own grief. I treated him like a well-meaning outsider. I allowed him to take care of me and then resented him for it. Oh, you know some of this. We're too alike, you and I. There's too big a crowd when we're together. Sam is something simpler, and I think I can be simpler with him, too. You ask too much, and you make me ashamed of my stinginess. I'm ashamed of myself now, writing this to you. But I'm not ashamed of trying again with Sam. It seems a way out—and we've both been stuck too long.

Forgive me.

Anne

But it's a good idea your getting away for a while," she said.

"He *is* away," Michael said, "he's away now. How far away does he have to get?"

"It'll be good to see Dinah, catch up with her."

"For Christsake, don't hang around Florence, will you?"

"I don't think so."

"I shouldn't tell you this, of course, but there's no way Sam and Anne are going to last."

"No?"

"You can't go back like that, like nothing's happened."

"According to Anne, nothing has."

They sat in the kitchen. Margaret Thatcher's voice wafted over the kedgeree. She told them to be realistic in their expectations, she told them not to be greedy, she said there was plenty for everyone if everyone would only hold back a little and think of others. Michael shut her off and ordered the boys to bed.

"I'm truly sorry it hasn't worked out," Helen said, "I don't know what she's doing."

Sounds of struggle came from upstairs, then Michael descended, purposeful.

"Is there anything you want us to do while you're gone?"

He mentioned the mail, his and Rachel's. She wrote it down.

He didn't envy them any longer, the fact that they were still together. They seemed old to him, and he seemed old to himself.

"Well," Michael said to him when they were alone, "I'm sorry you got hurt. You know that, don't you?"

"Of course."

"I don't take pride in having warned you, either."

"No."

"I was rooting for you."

"Come on, Michael."

"I wanted one of us to bring it off."

"What?"

"That's right. I don't mean Anne, I mean *it*. Whatever *it* is. I wanted one of us to bring it off. I thought you'd be the one."

"Me? Old shaky? You thought I'd be the one?"

"Yeah. Those that ask sometimes get. Those that don't ask . . ."

"What are you saying? You mean you don't think you asked?" Zach turned around in case Helen was returning.

"No, I don't think I asked. I think I thought I was doing

167

that, I really did, but I don't, nope, don't think I really asked. Of course, you didn't get, either."

"Michael, you got—look." He waved his arm wildly about him.

"I've got the work and the house and the boys, but the rest: I think we might be equal, buddy. I won't ever say this again, and I want you to strike it from the record, but I think if I start to measure the way you measure, I'd say that, I'd have to say it." Michael wasn't looking at him, but at his shoes, the office sneakers.

"And I might say a little more. I might say that however bad you feel about Anne or Maggie, at least you had it for a time."

"Not with Anne."

"You had it with Maggie. Sure, it didn't last, but it's something. To have been there."

"Wait a second. You think there's a difference here?" Again he raised the indicating arm.

"Sometimes that's what I think. Yes. Sometimes I wish I had what my brother has."

"Your brother, Michael, has nothing. One suitcase, and frankly, a great deal of pain. Your brother, Michael, is afraid he may be exiled for life, if you want to know."

"But my brother asks at least, even now, all these years later."

He held her blue pages in his hand, lay on Rachel's bed, and read them again:

We have lived everywhere, Zach and I. This city is haunted by where we've been, he and this I who is I no longer. He does not know me, this new man. I am ten and live with my parents and Tom. I am sixteen and have the lead in my school play. I am twenty-six walking here on this sidewalk with my handsome young husband and my beautiful child. She stops to look at the Easter ducks in the window. We stop and kiss on the street, with the unconsciousness that held us together for so many years, before the consciousness came, the years of self-definition and anger. And then it's gone, and I am thirty-six again, and we talk about other things. About who owns the city, for example.

Episcopalian feet patrol the east shore of Fifth Avenue. Elegant crones, spindly legged in springtime furs cane-tap their way through patches of sun this April Fool's Day. Dogs, joggers, the antique bird-ladies travel perilously among them. By May the dark furs will be in storage and out will come the lavender-gray suits and fox-headed tippets. In the summer the ladies will be gone. In the winter they are hardly visible. They are hardly ever here, a few weeks in autumn, and either side of Easter. I will not be an old lady like these, the ones that flow so gracefully into graciousness, content with the rare and elaborate family visits, Thanksgiving in town, July Fourth at the summer places with their lawns down to the water. The era that they are the end of holds out beyond expectation, thanks to kind doctors, loyal servants, the blind eye turned upon the rich. Not an easy life, but an uncomplaining one. Perhaps a sense of place. Who owns the city? David and I walking. Only the rich, he says, and the ones that still hang on to their little hoards, rent-controlled rooms, inherited co-ops. My time's limited here, he says, even the rent on my fast-food-reeking walk-up's too much. I, too, think of bag ladies and project. It's guilt, they say. All women who earn their living outside the rules imagine their futures this way, as outcasts economically, socially. Like the old fears of death through abortion for an afternoon's free love. Nothing free about it.

Passing the front door of what used to be our home, I feel the exclusion, though it was Zach who went. And passing the place I lived longest with Tom, where he died, the little balconied top floor, our home where the cats sat in the sun among the geraniums, I certainly feel the loss. I've avoided this journey for the last two years. Briefly I try to connect, but respectful of my present companion, we hardly linger. Nevertheless, it follows us down, this sense of loss.

April Fool's Day. We come upon the first games of the season, a dry, thawed, soon-to-be-dusty, green field in Central Park. Who owns the city? These guys do, surely, still. "Way to go," they say, and "Send it home." Suddenly my companion, my artist friend is back in *his* childhood: "No hitter here," he calls to the pitcher, a player's voice from out of his Soho-chic black and whites. Some things are costumes and some things are precious and you don't know which is which. My home with Zach was our precious costume. Who owns this town? Farther down, two black boys on moving carpets of air glide for the *culturati* by the steps of the Met. The white-faced mime juggles, his crowd around him. David and I speak of public spaces, Italian mostly. We have both been elsewhere, we are both here now. This fact confuses, somehow links us. Choosing it—New York—does not seem after all for those who know, say, the Piazza Navona, an absolute necessity. Yet we do choose, for no reason more intelligent than that we were children here: baseball terms and memories of public school, the system of bells, for example, that even now makes no period of concentration longer than forty minutes. Bells, hall scuffles, sneaker slapping, banging locker doors, all change. An ad on a bus goes by, tells you that the Ringling Brothers are in town again. Spring circuses, my birthday treat throughout the fifties, Karen's the past ten years. But it's different now, too much glitter, not enough tack. For example, the freak show, the best part, has been excised by humanitarian public demand. It's just sex now and cruelty to animals.

We walk all the way down through the park and then further through the canyons, all the way to the bottom of the island to his studio. I searched for wholeness all day, tried to put the fragments back together, connect them by walking through each place, myself the link, at least myself still here, despite all the selves dead and gone that still hurt like amputations. Zach, above all, myself with Zach, and him with Karen. The walk through the fragments ends in David's fragment-celebrating studio, among the collages.

We look at these for a while and then come out again—out on to the waterfront in the late spring light, before the boys take over the docks. A lot of street kids and two girls with their pedigreed dogs, everybody dirty from being out all day in the sunshine, and a darkening river barge creeping up, almost but in the end *not* unseen. And then the light on those red-brick warehouses with their golden panes of glass, reflecting all of us. The cars on the highway move through fast after the weekend, home to Brooklyn and Long Island, a fast stop at the lights. They look over to where we are, take us in in pieces, then move on in speed, getting the blurred and shattered images. Standing there, I didn't feel the losses any longer, only how it all becomes whole. How if you don't ask for things you sometimes get them, how if you don't demand wholeness in New York you sometimes get it, cobbled, the sum of the parts and more, as with David a gift of seeing if not having, better than having because it can't be taken back. Or not so easily.

Maggie's sense of loss, that much he hadn't guessed. He didn't remember the day they kissed in the street when Karen looked at the ducks. But she came back to him whole, nevertheless, in the clothes of a decade ago, sitting on the edge of the bathtub one evening in summer, splashing the baby, soaped and greasy and pink. He had stood watching them from the doorway, listening to the baby babble, looking at Karen and the blue duck that wobbled in the water, the water opaque with the scum of an Ivory Soap bar. Karen's black hair pinned up over her pink ears, wet strands of it coming down onto her fat shoulders. Maggie's peacefulness watching and stirring the water in the warmth of that evening. Karen patting the water with a flat little hand and talking in her peculiar language both to mother and duck, assured that she would be so befriended all her days.

Of course, it was his own youth he mourned then, too, in that evening that would never come back for them, all those evenings, the hours after Karen was in bed, when they cooked for one another, went to bed together, woke up together, took so much for granted. Let no man put asunder. Well, no man had. Only life, life had sundered them, robbed them, stolen away their happiness: her happiness, his happiness, the innocence of all three.

Was it really too late? Such triple devastation was an outrage, not to be taken so easily, mutely, courteously. A last struggle surely was the least that was due so much lost love.

He picked up the phone and gave the number, listened as the crisp English voice encountered the slow one, repeated its requirements patiently, accepted the superfluous greeting, and then somewhat snidely informed him he was through.

She was surprised by the call and the hour. He apologized and she waited. He tried to say the truth, but it wouldn't travel so far, under the ocean, over the static, into her present. She spoke instead, out of her evening, her fatigue, the meaningless events of her day. Meaningless because what he wanted was so much more urgent. He spoke from another day long ago, and willed her to hear it. *Because love doesn't vanish so easily*. Wanted her to throw away the years and the miles between them, push through space and time to the truth of that ancient moment of their being together.

It took a while before she understood, before her voice formed its edge, its querulousness, its compassion, then, and refusal. I inhabit the present, it declared to him, and I'm comfortable here. I thought by now, it said, you would have understood. At least that much. *It is over.*

When traveling, he saw in transparent pieces the insides of things, saw life in its natural glide, slipping past like amoeba under a microscope: fields, tunnels, people saying good-bye. Signs bearing the name of stations on his trip from Pisa brought him to a sense of where he was, how he was going on, moving in time, how his self and his life were separate, how the one carried the other like luggage. If he were a changed man as he had foolishly hoped, he could go home again. He could even pick up the remains of his life, reenter with new life, even his old job. Certainly it had seemed a possibility: what else is traveling but a bid to strengthen the heart? But he could not move, only a side step, the smallest manuever was open to him: a visit to Dinah, postcards for Karen, the pose of the purposeful daddy. He saw himself as he must seem: pushing his life along like a peanut, on all fours and in the dust, with the screams of disappointed children in the background.

Nevertheless, outside his own life, the continuity of things was pacifying, both what was permanent and the way humans buzzed and circulated in the face of that. On the station in Pisa they had tried to sell him leaning towers, battery-operated for bedtime reading, or flattened and stamped on headscarves to keep out the rain. Yet despite these attempts to reduce and possess it, the tower remained, a monument to be entered and climbed, or silently, royally gawped at.

He was paralyzed, that was the nature of it. In movement, the illusion of freedom slipped. The image of the knot grew clear: unravel or choke. His only happiness lay in renunciation.

The train brought him to Florence, to the station with the red carts of fruit and chocolate, kiosks with newspapers in every language. Above the travelers, the girders rose, catching light and smoke in the lace; steam from the trains billowed and mingled with the fog and drizzle of the town.

His taxi dieseled and honked through streets named for princes and architects, bore him through the rain along the river, rising now, mustard colored, in the autumnal floods. He carried his suitcase into an alleyway and through a small market square where odors of spoiling vegetation and grease from a *rosticceria* wafted about him, and pigeons circled and fluttered above. He found his sister's building and entered a chilly courtyard. Her name, in all its American uprightness, sat on a business card by the buzzers, pinned under filigreed brass, neighbored by the more exotically described, the *professori* and *baroni*. The building sloped around its stairway, dusty and cat-ridden. Following a shaft of light, he climbed to the top floor and proceeded to the end of a marble hallway where a door was open. He knocked gently and pushed with his suitcase, calling for her. There was no sound from inside. He stepped in, lifted aside a red velvet curtain, and found himself in a large north-lit room facing some twenty young men and women seated on stools and drawing in charcoal the scene before them. They stared upward, not at him, whom they barely registered, but at the person beside him, posed in front of the hanging, a gangly red-bearded youth, long-haired and naked, gray-fleshed as an oyster, with the raw blue feet of a disciple and the marks of a needle on his arms and neck.

No one spoke as Zach stood there, gazing about him in the reverential scratching silence. He adjusted his eyes to the light and located Dinah, sitting at the back, signaling him to silence.

There was something strange about the group before him, the women with long straight hair and pale American faces, wearing printed skirts, and the men, bearded, curly haired, in corduroy and leather sandals. They glowed, as though worshipping as they sketched, like a pre-Raphaelite community, or something older. Yes, that was it, they had made themselves, in their devotion, into a species of art. They had fused with the place, and the spirit of virtue and beauty that sustained it.

The session ended. They gathered their chalks and their shoulder bags and moved silently out of their trances. They spoke in low voices as they proceeded to the door, still moved by their communion. They smiled shyly at the model, who

unbending now, stretched, put on his jeans and lit a cigarette. Not until he was gone did Dinah speak.

"Zach," she said to him, reaching up to kiss him on both
cheeks, "imagine the train being on time. How was the
flight?"

"Good. What was all that?"

"The Saturday afternoon life class. I should have warned
you."

She busied herself stacking the little stools, hid them
behind long velvet curtains, waved her arm to indicate the
view. "Well, what do you think?"

The red tiles of the rooftops warped and tilted away from
them, and from the little square he had crossed to get there.
Behind were fifteenth-century towers, orange and crumbly
like a cake-bake model of Manhattan. On the roofs, in the
near distance, cats patrolled among the laundry lines, tip-
toed along the water gutters, on the lookout for birds.

"Now come and see upstairs." She led him up a short
flight of narrow cylindrical steps where the top of the apartment building led into a tower. "That's where Giorgio and
I sleep," she said, "you're above us."

"Giorgio?"

"Yes."

Another short flight up was an identical bedroom, its
corners stacked with black portfolios and drawing boards,
paperbacks and empty liters of wine. Dinah had laid a mattress in the middle of the stone floor and set a bottle of dried
flowers next to it.

"The bathroom's all the way down, still it's something
after New York, isn't it?"

"London."

"All the more so, then; how's Michael?"

She gave him supper, naming the ingredients, correcting his pronunciation, singing the praises of local foods, and of Giorgio, or George as she sometimes called him, he being, like most of her friends here, an American artist.

"And what do these people live on?" Zach asked.

"Money from home, a little teaching, a few sales. Some of them have to sell on the streets or make portraits of tourists. Just now, things are lean, but the summer's usually good. Anyway, you know what this place costs me? Three hundred dollars a month. You know what I'd get in New York for that? Space in a flophouse. Maybe you should hole up here for a while, do some real work, expose yourself to something important for a change."

"Important?"

"The Renaissance, for example. It's still all here, Zach. Art that is not just beauty, but something they haven't known in New York for a long time, beauty with conviction."

"I see."

"No more anxiety. No more doubt. If you stay here, it all rubs off. I want you to look at something."

She led him, excited and serious as a child, downstairs to the wall where Giorgio's work was hung: portraits of old men in red chalk, studies of placid young girls, self-portraits, staring, broody, bearded, the lines fierce and precise, the draftsmanship decisive.

"Let's see yours," Zach said, putting his arm around her.

"Oh, I'm nowhere near as good. That's mine up there, and that one, the small one."

"I'm afraid I like yours better," he said, "more of Dinah in it."

"Meaning what?" she said.

"You," Zach said, "your personality, your high spirits, not to mention color."

"I'm not trying to express my personality," she said shortly. "I'm trying to serve something else, the place for example, what's actually around me."

"Well, forgive me, when does Giorgio get back?"

"Later."

Later, Giorgio arrived, boomed in like an old salt, a little barrel-chested, merry with drink, corduroy-covered, and twinkly. He was a powerful man, squat and somewhat bull-necked, with heavy, unwavering brown eyes and a trim, white-flecked beard, burly and playful as the man who had once come to his kindergarten to sing "Jimmy Crack Corn" to a circle of sticky-handed infants.

He launched in as soon as he found the wine, set the bottle on the floor, knees wide apart to pull the cork, poured it out splashing over the sides of the goblets he'd lined up for them, began at once on tales of friends, community scandals. There was musical bedding in Florence, it seemed, and much mirth at that, infinite combinations of the principals, mostly American, the odd Italian or Frenchman among them, though these were quick to retreat, bettered, had. Giorgio, himself, as he revealed, had fathered five, parked at the moment up the hill in Fiesole, threatening to descend, or run home to Nebraska.

They drank until Zach could no longer feel his legs, and

then they laughed at him, let him go to bed, promising him adventures and brilliant companions for the nights that followed. Giorgio leaned over him, as he lay him on the mattress, whispered a sour-breathed *benvenuto fratello*, and kissed him good-night.

It was an odd time to be in Florence. Daily the sky was dark and the streets flooded with rain. In the mornings Dinah took him to the churches and museums and lectured him on the city's history. The weather and the buildings oppressed him, and the constant vividness of the past. He began to imagine assassins lurking in alleyways, the cries of unfavored princes rising through the grates of the dark palazzi that loomed over the narrow streets and shut out any light there was.

At lunchtime, Giorgio often joined them, his nails blackened by the morning's effort, and they would sit in greasy steam to eat the autumnal Florentine food: heavy dishes of lentils and sausage, *piccione*, *porcini*, consumed with glass after glass of the thick *"nero."*

In the afternoons, Dinah worked or held her sketch classes, while Zach sat upstairs with his guide books, composing postcards to the sounds of scratching and timid coughing that came from below. In the evenings, they took him to parties, where the same pale and solemn artists turned merry and lecherous under the effects of wine, poured endlessly from straw-wrapped casks. Till the early hours they romped and shouted, leered and groped. Untempted and out of place, Zach apologized to his hosts, and went to bed alone.

*   *   *

"Here's how paranoia happens in New York," Giorgio lectured him as he sat. "By chance you enter a shop in a neighborhood where a large building has been cordoned off by the police. Someone asking questions at the counter makes you curious. You inquire and find there has been an accident, in this case, a fall from the top of the building, a woman's death. It strikes you that had you not been needing to buy coffee you would not have entered this shop; if you had not just visited your friend you would not be in this neighborhood with the police car and the cordoned-off building. Since you just happen to be in this area, it occurs to you as a possibility that similar accidental deaths have been happening throughout the city, discussed over the counter in many different shops.

"You wonder whether this death will be reported on the TV news. When it isn't, you wonder if it will be mentioned in the paper. In the morning you forget to buy the paper, but you remember the death. Gradually you are convinced that in this city people drop, their deaths censored, like flies."

The invitation had been bandied about for days, so that it was merely a matter of time before Giorgio had Zach sitting in faked composure on a velvet armchair, his face to the light that came intermittently between the Florentine clouds, as Giorgio sketched him.

"I am creating in you a portrait of the city man," he told him. "You have all the comforts of that life and no contentment. Damn this light. It is impossible to work under such conditions."

From time to time, Dinah would approach to investigate the progress of the work. She refrained from commenting directly, but Zach could see in the quick movement of her eye from the paper to his face a shared training and purpose with Giorgio.

"I do not like his mouth," Giorgio said to her, "I do not like his mouth at all."

When he could forget the discomfort of his pose, Zach let his mind wander in and out of Giorgio's amiable monologue.

"I am not one of your lovers of the present," he said to him, "but I will let you represent it. In the lines of your brow and the tension of your mouth, I see its toll. But you're something of a fighter, aren't you? If you weren't, you'd be a faceless man of the city, and then I couldn't draw you. As it is, you display your struggles in your features, in your posture, in the dead droop of your legs. This is all very interesting. It's been a while since I had a fresh New Yorker to pin on paper. They come through, you know, and buzz around and think they might like to work here. But they seldom stay, they return to the Apple and become men of commerce."

He scratched heavily with his charcoals, blew on the paper, dabbed at it with a little cloth. His brow contracted with the effort.

"By commerce, I don't necessarily mean they give up painting. They become New York career artists, working for dealers, eyeing each other in fancy restaurants, grieving over party invitations. I did it myself for six years, I know all about it. And then I discovered something. Shall I tell you what it was?"

Zach kept his pose and his silence as instructed.

"I discovered that the linear notion of art is simply a tyranny. Because I was born after Cézanne, must I paint accordingly? What if I choose to end my art history somewhere around 1600, where's the illegality in that? No, let Picasso praise Cézanne for his anxiety, myself I simply turn my chair and my back on it. Look at you, you have enough anxiety for both of us."

"You simply refuse to accept the present?" Zach asked him.

"Don't move. Certainly. And here nothing forces me to do so. It's a museum, isn't it, Florence? A very special museum. Let other fools capture the look of the subways and the atomic bomb. I shall paint faces that cannot be dated with any accuracy. My endeavor, immodest as it is, is to slip out of time. By evasion I shall triumph."

"The present is where you live," Zach mentioned.

"Hold still. Florence is where I live. Not at all the same thing. Very pleasant, Florence. And actually not so easy to be an artist here, given how pleasant it is. Or at least not easy for the natives. My theory is there are so many artists in New York because "real life" is so hostile, easy enough to abandon for the solace of the studio. And the isolation necessary to make art is only a small step beyond the daily ordeal. Whereas here and in England the mesh of cozy humanity is so tight around one, for good or ill—I think of D. H. Lawrence and Auden among the many claustrophobics—that to break free, choose solitude, is a radical act. Hence the continuing perceived menace of the avant-garde; hence the preference, in English letters at least, for literature that still lovingly affirms connection, embraces or satirizes or rails against social life. But American art, that is the great Instead. It is made out of the deprivations of solitude, rage at the inadequacies. Or to put it another way: New York is a desert and its art is made of the mirages."

"And here?"

"And here I have an expatriate's privacy for my work and a beautiful ancient city for my pleasure. Perfectly arranged, isn't it?"

"If you are willing to ignore modern art and contemporary life."

"But that is one way of being an artist, my friend, because an artist is simply one who is greedy for power (spurious of course) over the facts of his existence. The desire to escape is one of the great constants of art, not only the escape from what is heartrendingly ordinary or brutal, but another more fundamental evasion. Why else does the modern artist continually transform his style except for fear of being identified and therefore defined? Of course, some artists stop and repeat themselves, the better to be understood and loved for that easy recognition. A real artist, however, is not motivated by the desire to be loved, but by what may be its opposite: the desire to be free, to evade both constraint and detection."

"But not you," Zach said. "You choose to escape by living

in a city and aesthetic of the past, one that has nothing to do with your own."

"Especially not my own. All right, move. Certainly not my own. What an idea. What else is freedom for but to get rid of the circumstances one was born with?"

"And submit yourself to someone else's world?"

"Freedom is like money, Zach, it has no value in itself, only in what it can be exchanged for. Get your money's worth, I say. Too many people go to the fair, come back with shoddy goods, shiny stuff that shrinks in the rain. Keep it in your pocket, but not too long, you'll end up with pockets full of paper, and outrage at closing time."

"I doubt it's so finite," Zach said, getting up.

"There challenges a patriot," Giorgio mocked him, "from the land of the free, land of the people who value freedom of and for itself: opportunity. To do what? To make more money. To buy more freedom. No, freedom was given to us to give away."

"And this is what you've exchanged it for?" Zach asked.

"For the moment, yes."

"The moment?"

"Well, as you know," Giorgio said, winking at him, "I, too, am an American."

He was a natural father, Giorgio, despite his abandoned children in the hills, or perhaps in compensation. He led Dinah and Zach about the streets with a kindly parental air, showing Zach where the best stationers were, the best *vinicoli*, the best view of the bridges. Dinah was devoted to him, and obedient to all his hints and suggestions. Her sufferings were confined to her art, which she submitted to the shadow of his own, and to his pronouncements: "To the Renaissance we owe the discovery that man does not need Christ to justify his existence, nor the presence of Jupiter to make him strong and beautiful. His grace is within him, buried in his thorax, sternum, and solar plexus. We have only to see it again and set it down to retrieve him from the dishonor into which he has fallen." So Dinah would strive with her brushes and charcoal to resurrect the fallen angel, sighing and whimpering as she worked, rubbing out the lines of doubt and weakness that were natural to her, editing out and peering inward until, transcending the abject circumstances of her models—large-eared Australian tourists, crater-skinned American vets, and sullen hippies—she isolated the nobility of her subject and declared the greater truth.

Likewise she imposed starry blinkers on her relations with Giorgio. Just as she deformed the natural tendencies of her art towards color and looseness, until it most resembled the dark and authoritative definitions of his, so she altered herself so she could fit in with the imagined ideals of her man. She spoke an incessant and flamboyant Italian, accompanied Giorgio in his drinking, parodied his booming laughter with her own, and swapped almost as man to man the ribald anecdotes that were current fashion among their group of friends.

Yet under the *Bohème* manner and robustness, Zach thought he saw still the delicate hesitant woman who was his sister, who seemed to him to have exchanged something crucial for this pantomime life of "conviction."

"How long have you been so Italian?" he asked, after a day in which she had rolled the exotic vowels for him, not only in contact with the Florentines, but to him, pointing out the sights, naming the street signs, instructing him on local color and use.

"It feels like forever."

"And you'll never come home?"

"I am home."

"I mean America."

"I can't live there, I couldn't possibly. Look at this place. Where in America is there a street like this one?"

"You never found New York beautiful?"

"I hate it."

"And the language, you don't miss that? Your whole childhood's there. That counts, doesn't it? This is so much later for you, Dinah, how can it really be yours? And what's Giorgio up to with his family? What do you think about that, eh?"

"I don't think about it. It's not my business."

"Dear Dinah, when did you begin to ask so little?"

"Little? I have my work, and a place I love, and a man I love. What's little about that?"

"Then why don't I recognize you in any of this at all?"

"Oh, that's so American. You mean authenticity, don't you, or do you mean narcissism? Or maybe it's just the same."

"All right, authenticity. There is something pathetic about these expatriates making old master drawings, selling caricatures of tourists on the steps of the Uffizi. Why don't they all go home? What are they doing in this weather?"

"You mean, why don't you go home, don't you?" Dinah asked him. "I can see that you can't, but I don't know what's preventing you. I don't know why you're so footloose and heavyhearted at the same time. One or the other, Zach, but not both."

His bodily loneliness was acute, all the more so watching the devotees of art grope and giggle on the makeshift couches and daybeds that lined their different rooms, there where parties raged from one high pitch to another until the early hours of morning, fueled by plentiful cheap wine and the rock music of twenty years before. Watching the art students, the married men and pale, earnest young girls, their tongues in and out of each other's ears and mouths as they gripped one another on the dance floor, or in candle-lit corners of a room, he was oppressed by the activity of the scenes, by their urgency and lightness. The young girls in their jeans and flowered dresses interested him not at all, but he felt his body useless and heavy around him. He longed to rid himself of it, into the body of another, to throw it away in such fashion, give it up to someone else, someone other than his solely self-possessing, all too familiar self.

He walked at night, in long angry strides along the Arno, listening to the waters slipping and churning on the stone below the sidewalk, under the bridges. He walked hatless in the misty rain that gusted around corners and bathed the cobblestones in reflected streetlight. Bodies came towards him, singly or in couples. Sometimes, female, they beseeched him, offered to slow him down, jeered at him as he passed. He might have stopped, but his loneliness drove him on to exorcism by the speed of his walking, as though he could walk to the end of it, by passing just so many bridges, just so many squares, as though he could take himself home three hours later, thus exhausted, and no longer need to find what was missing.

Late one night, coming towards the Excelsior Hotel, where the girls were usually plentiful, leaning against the wall of the hotel, standing in single file some eight feet apart, chatting over this scrupulous distance, instantly alert when a car pulled up or a patron sauntered, wifeless, out among them, he noticed the wall empty but for a single figure, who watched him in his furious progress along the riverwalk. For his benefit she put herself under a street lamp, and sang to him sotto voce the usual endearments.

Perhaps because of the hour, perhaps because she was alone, perhaps because of his anger as great as his loneliness, he crossed to where she was, took from her the cigarette she proffered, discussed a price, surprisingly low—the Almighty Dollar he supposed—and came to an agreement. She walked five paces ahead of him, enough to let him assess the line of ass and legs under her short leather skirt. Her hair was tossed over the side of her head, her sweater, despite the November cold, fell over one shoulder, Rita Hayworth style. She led him, always at a six-feet distance, through the deserted back streets by the Piazza Goldoni, until they reached the door of her apartment. Here she paused and handed him the key, in sudden deference to the courtesies of the male. Once inside she kissed him and held him with her own slight, muscular body, pulling his shirt from his belt, unzipping him there in the hallway, bending now on her knees to take him in her mouth, pushing her hands against his thighs, moaning all the while her Italian moans, brushing him with her hair, baring her teeth and tongue, bowing before him like a slave and dealing with him like a predator.

She led him to her room—the door unlocked, the bed unmade—and pushed him onto the bed where he tried to undress her. With one arm, she held him back, undressing herself, first the sweater and skirt. And here he sat up, because under the sweater and bra, under the skirt and lace panties, under the black strap of garter, there showed the unmistakable lines—beautiful as the David—but nevertheless the lines of a male.

He rose speechless, and now so angry he was in danger of hurting her. Him. His arm rose and she cringed. Then she came at him again, stroking him, soothing him with her voice. He pushed her off. "No," he said, his outrage ridiculous even to himself.

"*Ma non capisco.*"

"You're a man," he said, still baffled by it.

"*Ma é chiaro,*" she said, pleading, explaining. "You don't get a woman so cheaply." She repeated the price to him. "That is the price of a man," she told him. "Come," she said, "it's almost as good as the real thing."

He didn't make the effort again. He confined himself to walks on the other side of the river, and to long stays in his room. At dawn the pigeons woke him, babbling and cooing their nursery noises. They inhabited the room with him, nesting in the holes in the stone that had been sealed off with little squares of glass. Through these he watched them, the mothers sitting on their eggs, hatching out the pigeon young, pink and gray as rats, which craned wrinkly necks, opened and shut their beaks, and pushed their blind heads into the air when the mothers left them, off for food or straw on expeditions into town. When the adults were away, Zach watched the infants that lived in the holes in the wall, anxious for them when the mothers were gone too long, both repelled and curious. Equally curious to him was the fact that not once in his life had he ever seen a baby pigeon, in or out of its egg. Aviary family life had all gone on somewhere among the many corners of New York invisibility. Still, he hadn't missed much—they were unspeakably ugly baby birds.

He lay on his bed composing postcards. He sent Karen Fra' Angelico's angels, the images carefully scrutinized for the presence of martyrs, that omnipresent lineup lurking modestly in even the most ethereal compositions: St. Stephen, wearing on his head a stone like a pancake, and graphically oozing blood, ditto St. Martin with hatchet-embedded crown. Like the seven dwarfs, the ghoulish clique stood in line and accompanied the Virgin and her fluffier throng.

To Michael and Helen he sent sunset views of the Duomo with cheerful comments on his own and Dinah's health and happiness. And to both Maggie and Anne, in conscious parody of his own pain, he sent Masaccio's famous image of expulsion from Paradise.

In Florence he was able to lose both London and New York, but not proceed. By the cultural Disneyland he was only partly enchanted. Enchantment held his sister, however, together with the rubicund troll that guarded the castle. If occasionally he wondered about Giorgio's former life, he kept his curiosity to himself, unwilling to hear the bouncy declarations of spiritual freedom that would greet his questions. His own simpler paternity weighed on him, however—his proposed absence at Christmas, indeed his present, apparently endless, absence from "home." Yet going back increasingly seemed a wrongheaded excursion. He knew something must change, yet beyond change of address he did not know where such change would come from, dealing now in solitude, present but unconnected in other people's lives, rattling there like a single marble in a tin box. Setting out months ago, it had been his intention to get *in*, and so he still might, take up one of the expatriate girls, rent a piano and a *piano nobile*, and exchange remarks on pre-Cubist painting with Giorgio over a candle and a fiasco of red wine.

But it would be false for him to enter into so much falseness. He clung stubbornly to a ragged notion of what might be true. No, you could not just transplant yourself anywhere like a yam. There were always conditions of growth. The city began to stultify him. He began to detect something sinister in the place and in the fatuous rompings of the exiles, with their colored chalks and feverish couplings, their bottomless vats of Chianti and posturings of bohemia. Perhaps it was only that inside a grotesque construction of Old-World life, they parodied New York disconnection in their vaunts of freedom and light-handed use of one another. Or perhaps their familyless and frantic sexual lives so depressed him only because they mocked his own. Not only fatuous, their world now struck him as irredeemably bleak, based on a few chilly and antiquated notions. In his mind, dampened in Florence, he conjured up warmer scenes of Helen with Mick and Willis around their oak table, listening to the sweet or sour paternal banter of his brother Michael. And inside that scene, of course, a decade of Christmas mornings with Maggie and Karen.

He watched himself in an aspect of his sister, saw how she, too, needed to get *in*, into Giorgio's certainties and into the Renaissance, wrap its "beauty with conviction" feathers around her and there sue for peace. Conviction, wouldn't that be something for these children of the anxious culture?

But just how did they get so lonely? What had parented them, that they could parent so little? An ordinary New England couple, abandoned after the moral certainties of World War II to a changed and confusing world, a world of rewards for nothing in particular, except historical good luck, to have been there and not here. It was given and they partook, and yet they had imparted unease to their brood in such measures that two had hidden themselves in the Old World and one was wandering still, looking for home, snuffling like a piglet for the elusive tit.

Snuffling and then choking, too, and seemingly forever strung between the two responses, asking and refusing, declaring yes and declaring no. And here, particularly, watching himself say *no, no* to trouping round the streets of Florence in snippets of velvet and tapestry like medieval minstrels, in corduroy and beards like cheap Puccini, *no* to mouthing Italian syllables like wads of bubble gum, an incantation to keep the American facts away, *no* to someone else's Renaissance—he who needed his own. In his own refusals he began to catch an echo of theirs, both Maggie's and Anne's, and to accept. *No* was the word he must practice before he could say yes. Wandering the museums, he had seen room after room of the icon, those hundreds of *madonne coi bambini*, the holy unions that must be shattered.

Gone. He was stuck between the mourning and the need to go himself. He was stuck before the task: the need to make out of deprivation a salute of farewell. He needed to open his hand and let it go, everything that was already gone. And then, and only then, to begin again.

One evening, returning to his room, he saw that the birds in their stone nests had simply disappeared.

"But they were too young to fly," he said to Dinah, "and there were too many of them."

"Then the hawks must have gotten them," she said. "They come sometimes. Count yourself lucky it happened while you were away."

"How can she have anxiety attacks, she's only thirteen years old?"

They were sitting on plastic seats in the Heathrow passenger lounge, waiting for Karen's delayed flight from New York. In little pockets of tranquility, between the gift-burdened rushing for planes, Indian women in nylon bloomers pushed cigarette packets and candy papers into neat piles with their brooms.

"And after she goes, you'll stay?" Michael asked.

"Since there's no reason to go back."

"How long are you going to live like this?" Michael asked him.

"What do you suggest?"

"What do I suggest? If I suggest anything you're going to do something else. You know Anne didn't work it out with Sam, I could always suggest that."

"How come?"

"What I said to begin with, there's no going back like that, it was a fantasy."

Helen had done it, but Zach didn't say so.

"So maybe you should give her a call," Michael said. "Anne and a piano should be enough for any man."

"The old Freudian solution," Zach said, "somewhat reduced. Anne and a piano."

"An era of reduced expectations. Take her to New York, take her to Venice, do something with her."

"You think?"

"Sure, give her a ring, invite her for Christmas. We'll have a big family Christmas, turkey and plum pudding for us and the kids and two bottles of whiskey for her. Invite her, it'll be fun."

"Nothing's that easy. What's gotten into you?"

"Why not? Everybody should have what they want for Christmas."

"I see. And what about the day after?"

"The day after's called Boxing Day here. That's the day you wrap all the leftovers, stick them in boxes, and give them away. Preferably to the poor."

"Right. You don't make turkey sandwiches. You clear out the larder and move on. Out with the old, in with the new."

"And one week later you sing 'Auld Lang Syne.' "

"Only under the influence. Listen, Anne's instincts are sound. She knew I wasn't a sure proposition. I'm hardly that now. I'm afraid it's all going to take a lot more time than I'd bargained for."

"Is that what you'll tell Karen?"

"She'll understand. She knows I'll be back when I can."

"And what exactly is it you're waiting for, if I may ask?"

"Maybe for nothing more than the sense of waiting to disappear, a little green light, a realization that all the little pieces have flown back together again, and I can resume my life."

"I've got news for you," Michael said a little sheepishly, "Helen's already invited Anne for Christmas and Anne has already accepted."

"They what?"

"Don't get excited, this is England. That sort of thing doesn't mean anything. Or not much. Or not much more than a sort of generalized goodwill."

"I see."

"It's all pretty easy, Zach, if you just don't think about it too hard. One way or another, this is all going to work out, and it doesn't much matter if you imagine yourself in charge or not."

The doors separating them from the arriving passengers opened suddenly and a stream of travelers emerged. Zach tapped Michael and together they walked towards the place where Karen was struggling with her luggage. Seeing them, she set down her bags, and opened her arms wide to embrace her father, just as though it were she who was welcoming him home.

About the Author

JANET HOBHOUSE was born in 1948 in New York City, where she lived until she went to England at the age of sixteen. She read English at Oxford University and returned to New York in 1971 when she began to write about art. In 1975 she published *Everybody Who Was Anybody: A Biography of Gertrude Stein*. She has written two other novels, *Nellie Without Hugo* and *Dancing in the Dark*.

Ms. Hobhouse is a contributing editor of *Art News* and a fellow of the New York Institute for the Humanities. She writes on theater for *Vogue* and is currently completing a study of the female nude in twentieth-century art. She lives in New York City.

VINTAGE
CONTEMPORARIES

VINTAGE
CONTEMPORARIES

"Today's novels for the readers of today."

— VANITY FAIR

"Real literature—originals and important reprints—in attractive, inexpensive paperbacks."

— THE LOS ANGELES TIMES

"Prestigious."

— THE CHICAGO TRIBUNE

"A very fine collection."
— THE CHRISTIAN SCIENCE MONITOR

"Adventurous and worthy."

— SATURDAY REVIEW

"If you want to know what's on the cutting edge of American fiction, then these are the books you should be reading."
— UNITED PRESS INTERNATIONAL